Julianne stared at Frank, dazed. "I just threw myself at you."

And he would have liked nothing more than to catch her. But he knew he wouldn't. Not if he wanted a clear conscience.

"Yes, you did."

"Oh." She felt naked and vulnerable. "You don't want me."

He laughed then and shook his head. God, was she ever off base.

"Lady, you are definitely not as good at reading people as you think you are." Because they were standing outside her hotel and not inside her room, he allowed himself a second more to drink in her presence, and all that could have been. "I don't think the word 'want' even *begins* to describe what I'm feeling right now."

Dear Reader,

Welcome back for another installment of the CAVANAUGH JUSTICE series. In this particular story, we meet Detective Frank McIntyre, the younger of Chief of Detectives Brian Cavanaugh's two stepsons. A ladies man from the cradle, Frank currently heads a task force to bring a real "lady killer" to justice. Detective Julianne White Bear from the Mission Ridge police department is sent to Frank and his crew to lend a hand when one of the serial killer's victims is discovered within that city's borders. The chemistry between Frank and Julianne is immediate—and so is her resistance. Secretly, all Julianne wants to do is find her missing, runaway cousin Mary, help solve the murders if she can and go back to Mission Ridge. Frank has some very different ideas about her agenda. It's a case of the irresistible force meeting the immovable object. Can some sort of an explosion be far behind?

As ever, I would like to thank you for reading and may love find you when you least expect it.

Best,

Marie Ferrarella

MARIE FERRARELLA

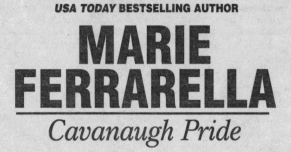

Cavanaugh Pride

Romantic
SUSPENSE

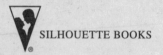

SILHOUETTE BOOKS

ISBN-13: 978-0-373-27641-7

CAVANAUGH PRIDE

Visit Silhouette Books at www.eHarlequin.com

Printed in U.S.A.

Books by Marie Ferrarella

MARIE FERRARELLA

This *USA TODAY* bestselling and RITA® Award-winning author has written more than one hundred and fifty books for Silhouette, some under the name Marie Nicole. Her romances are beloved by fans worldwide. Visit her Web site at www.marieferrarella.com.

To Jacinta, who lights up Nik's life
and made him smile again.

Chapter 1

Detective Julianne White Bear didn't want to be here. And she was sure the four detectives looking her way in the homicide squad room didn't want her here. They weren't openly hostile, but she knew resistance when she saw it.

She couldn't blame them. She knew all about being territorial and, if the tables were turned, she would have felt exactly the same way.

But Captain Randolph had sent her here and she wasn't about to argue with the man. Years before she joined the force, she had learned to pick her battles judiciously. When she did decide to dig in and fight, the very act carried an impact.

Besides, who knew? Maybe it was fate that brought her here. Maybe this was the place where she would finally find Mary. This was where her leads had brought her.

For a moment, Julianne silently scanned the small, crammed room, assessing its inhabitants. The lone woman looked to be about her age, maybe a couple of years older. She'd been talking to two men, both of whom had a number of years on her. The man off to the other side was younger.

He was also studying her.

She wondered which one of the detectives was in charge of the newly assembled task force and how long it would be before she butted heads with him—or her.

"Can I help you?" Detective Francis McIntyre, Frank to anyone who wanted to live to see another sunrise, asked the slender, dark-haired woman standing just inside the doorway.

His first thought was that a relative of one of the dead girls had finally shown up, but something about her had him dismissing the thought in the next moment. He couldn't deny that he'd be relieved if she wasn't. Though he'd been working homicide for a while now, breaking the dreaded news to people that their child, spouse, loved one was forever lost was something Frank knew he would never get used to.

Mentally taking a breath, Julianne crossed to the good-looking detective. A pretty boy, she thought. Probably used to making women weak in the knees. She didn't get weak in the knees. Ever. She knew better.

"Actually, I'm here to help you." Saying that, Julianne held out the folder she'd brought with her from Mission Ridge's small, single-story precinct. She was acutely aware she was being weighed and measured by the tall, muscular dark-haired man with the intensely blue eyes. A glance toward the bulletin board indicated the others were following suit.

"You have some information about the killer?" Frank asked, looking at her curiously as he took the folder from her.

Was the woman a witness who'd finally decided to come forward? God knew they needed a break. Something didn't quite gel for him. Most people who came forward, whether over the phone or in person, usually sounded a little uncomfortable and always agitated. This witness—if she *was* a witness—seemed very cool, very calm. And she'd obviously organized her thoughts enough to place them into a folder.

"No, those are my temporary transfer papers—plus all the information we have about our homicide."

"'Our'?" Frank repeated, flipping open the manila folder. He merely skimmed the pages without really reading anything. Three were official-looking papers from the human resources department from Mission Ridge, the rest had to do with a dead woman, complete with photographs. As if they didn't have enough of their own.

"I'm from Mission Ridge," she told him, pointing to the heading on the page he'd opened to. "Detective White Bear, Julianne."

He frowned.

"I don't know if we have any openings in the department," he began. "And besides, I'm not the person to see about that—"

Julianne's belief in the economy of words extended

to the people who took up her time, talking. She cut him off. "It's already been arranged. My captain talked to your chief of detectives," she told him. "A Brian—"

"Cavanaugh, yes, I'm familiar with the name."

Frank was more than familiar with the name and the man, seeing as how Brian Cavanaugh had been part of his life for a very long time, starting out as his mother's squad car partner. Just recently the man had married Frank's mother and made no secret of the fact that he was absorbing Frank, his brother, Zack, and two sisters, Taylor and Riley, detectives all, into what was by now the legendary Cavanaugh clan.

He would have expected a heads-up from Brian about this turn of events, not because he was his stepfather, but because Brian was his boss.

"And just why are you being transferred here?" he asked.

"*Temporarily* transferred." Julianne emphasized the keyword, then pointed to the folder. "It's all in there."

Frank deliberately closed the folder and fixed this unusually reticent woman with a thoughtful look. "Give me the audio version."

She smiled ever so slightly. "Don't like to read?" she guessed.

"Don't like curves being thrown at me." And this one, he couldn't help notice despite the fact that she was wearing a pantsuit, had some wicked curves as well as the straightest, blackest hair he'd ever seen and probably the most exotic face he'd come across in a long time. "Why don't you tell me why you're here?" he suggested.

"I'm here because my captain and your chief of detectives seem to think that the body we found in Mission Ridge the other night is the work of your serial killer."

Frank didn't particularly like the woman's inference that the killer was Aurora's exclusive property. That placed the responsibility for the killing spree squarely on their shoulders—the squad's and his.

Damn it, they should have been able to find the sick S.O.B. by now.

He was just being edgy, Frank upbraided himself. Edgy and overly tired. Ever since he had put two and two together and realized they had a full-fledged serial killer and had gotten his new stepfather to give him the go-ahead to put a task force together, he'd been working almost around the clock. As far as he was concerned, this was *his* task force and *his* killer to bring to justice. The fact that they were getting nowhere fast tended to rob him of his customary good humor.

"And why would they think that, White Bear, Julianne?" Frank asked, echoing the introduction she'd given.

Julianne didn't even blink as she recited, "Because the woman was found strangled and left in a Dumpster. There was no evidence of any sexual activity." To underscore what she was saying, she opened the folder he still held and turned toward the crime-scene photos. "That's where your killer puts them, isn't it? In a Dumpster?"

Both questions were rhetorical. Ever since Randolph had told her he was loaning her out to Aurora, she'd read everything she could get her hands on about the serial killer's M.O. Lamentably, there hadn't been much.

"He's not my killer," Frank corrected tersely.

"Sorry," she apologized quietly. There was no emotion in her voice. "No disrespect intended."

The blonde she'd first noticed standing by the bulletin board came forward, an easy smile on her lips. The first she'd seen since entering the room, Julianne noted.

"Don't mind Frank. He gets a little testy if he can't solve a crime in under forty-eight hours. To him life is one great big Rubik's Cube, meant to be aligned in record time. I'm Riley McIntyre," the woman told her, extending her hand. "This is my brother, Frank." Riley nodded toward the two men she'd been talking with. They were still standing by the large bulletin board. Across the top of the bulletin board were photographs. Each one belonged to a different woman who had fallen victim to the Dumpster killer. There were five photographs, each heading its own column. "That's Detective John Sanchez and Detective Lou Hill." Each nodded in turn as Riley introduced them.

Julianne saw the flicker of interest in their eyes. Assessing the new kid.

How many times had that happened in her lifetime? she thought. Enough to make her immune to the process, or so she wanted to believe.

Julianne nodded politely toward the two detectives, then looked back at the smiling, petite blonde. Despite her manner, Julianne had a feeling the woman could handle herself quite well if it came down to that. "And which of you is in charge?" she wanted to know.

"That would be me," Frank told her.

Of course it would, Julianne thought. She glanced at the folder he held. "Then maybe you'd like me to read that file to you?" she offered.

This one was going to be a handful, Frank thought. Just what he *didn't* need right now. "Riley, get your new little playmate up to speed," he instructed, heading for the door.

"Where are you going?" Riley asked, raising her voice.

Frank paused only to glance at her over his shoulder, giving his sister a look that said she should be bright enough to figure that out.

It was Julianne who was first to pick up on the meaning behind the expression. He was going to the chief of detectives, she would have bet a year's pay on it—and she wasn't one who gambled lightly.

"Before you go," she called out to him, "you should know that I don't want to be here as much as you don't want me here."

"Not possible," was all he said as he exited the squad room.

"Don't mind Frank," Riley told her again. "He hasn't learned how not to take each case he handles personally." She led Julianne over to the bulletin board to bring her up to speed. "Don't tell him I said so, but he's really not a bad guy once you get to know him. Authority has made him a lot more serious than he usually is," she explained. "He's still working things out."

Julianne had always believed that, up to a point, everyone was responsible for his or her life and the way things turned out. "If he's not comfortable with it, why did he agree to be in charge?"

"Because Frank was the first one who made the connection between the latest victim and the other bodies." She gestured toward the bulletin board. "Until then, they were on their way to becoming cold cases," Riley told her. "C'mon, I'll get you settled in first. This is a pretty nice place to work," Riley assured her with feeling, a smile backing up her words.

Julianne glanced over her shoulder toward the doorway where Frank had disappeared. She supposed she couldn't blame the man for being abrupt. She wasn't exactly thrilled about all this, either. "I'm willing to be convinced."

"An open mind," Riley commented with a wide grin. "Can't ask for more than that."

Julianne thought of Mary and all the months she'd spent trying to find her seventeen-year-old cousin— afraid that when she did find her, it might be too late— if it wasn't already.

"Yeah," Julianne answered quietly, "actually, you can."

The blonde spared her a curious look, but made no comment.

Frank knocked on Brian Cavanaugh's door. "Got a minute?"

He'd waited outside the glass office, curbing his impatience, while his new stepfather had been on the phone. But the moment the chief of detectives had hung up, Frank popped his head in, attempted to snare an island of the man's time before the phone rang again or someone walked in to interrupt them.

Brian smiled. This was an interruption he welcomed, even though he had a feeling he knew what it was about. He'd known Frank, boy and man, for almost as long as he'd known Lila and was proud of the way Frank and his siblings had turned out. They were all a credit to the department—as well as to their mother.

"For you? Always." Brian beckoned his stepson in and gestured toward one of the two chairs in front of his desk. "Take a seat."

About to demure, Frank changed his mind and sat down. He looked less confrontational sitting then standing, even if he preferred the latter.

"What's up?" Brian asked.

Frank didn't beat around the bush. "Did you assign a detective from Mission Ridge to my task force?"

Brian nodded. He'd guessed right, but he hadn't expected to see Frank in his office for at least a day or so. Had he and White Bear locked horns already? Had to be some kind of a record.

"I meant to tell you, but then the mayor called with another one of his mini-emergencies. With the police chief out on medical leave, I get to wear more than one hat." With the current mayor, however, it was more a case of constant placating and hand-holding. The mayor was highly agitated about the serial killer, afraid that if the man wasn't captured soon, it would bring down his administration when elections came around in the fall. "Don't know how Andrew took it for all those years," he added, referring to his older brother, who before taking early retirement to raise his five children had been Aurora's chief of police.

And then Brian took a closer look at Frank. If the young detective clenched his jaw any harder, his teeth would pop out.

"Why? Is something wrong? You did say you could use more of a staff."

"Yes, but I meant someone from *our* homicide

division." He'd never thought someone from the outside would be brought in. He didn't have time to integrate this woman. "Maybe Taylor, or—"

"Granted, we have the superior police department," Brian agreed, tongue in cheek. Mission Ridge's police department numbered twelve in all, but he'd been given White Bear's record and found it exemplary. "But I thought, since the captain called from Mission Ridge and the killer's M.O. was exactly the same as the serial killer we're dealing with, that it wouldn't hurt to bring in a fresh set of eyes." That said, Brian leaned back in his chair to study his stepson. "Is there a problem?"

Other than feeling as if he was being invaded, no, Frank thought, there wasn't a problem. At least, not yet. And then he replayed his own words in his head before speaking. He was coming across like some kind of grumpy malcontent.

Leaning back, Frank blew out a breath and then shook his head. "No, I guess I just would have liked a heads-up."

"Sorry I couldn't give you one," Brian apologized, then added, "I'm sure that the dead women would have liked to have been given a heads-up that they were about to become the serial killer's next victims."

"Point taken," Frank murmured. Brian was right. Nothing really mattered except clearing this case and getting that damn serial killer off the streets before he killed again. If bringing in some detective from a nearby town accomplished that, so be it. And then, because it was Brian, the man who used to bring him and his siblings toys when they were little, the man who he'd secretly wished was his father when he was growing up, Frank let down his guard and told him what was really bothering him. "I just thought that maybe you thought—"

"If I didn't think you were up to the job, Frank, I wouldn't have let you head up the task force," Brian informed him. "My marrying your mother has nothing to do with what I think of you as a law-enforcement officer. And if I have something to say about your performance, I won't resort to charades—or to undermining your authority. You know me better than that," he emphasized.

"Yeah, I do," Frank agreed, feeling just a little foolish for this flash of insecurity. This, too, was new to him. Self-confidence was normally something he took for granted.

"I hear that White Bear's good," Brian continued. "Maybe what she has to contribute might help you to wind up this case."

If only, Frank thought. Out loud, he said, "Maybe," and stood up, turning toward the door. He'd wasted enough of the chief's time.

"Frank?" Brian called after him.

Frank stopped and looked at the man over his shoulder. "Yes, sir?"

"Go home at a reasonable hour tonight," Brian instructed. "Get some sleep. You're no good to me—or anyone else—dead on your feet."

Frank turned to face him again. "I'm not dead on my feet," he protested.

They both knew he was, but Brian inclined his head, allowing the younger man the benefit of the charade. "Almost dead on your feet."

The last thing he wanted was preferential treatment.

There'd already been some talk making the rounds about that. Since his mother had married Brian, there'd been rumors sparked by jealousy. He was beginning to have new respect for what the younger Cavanaughs had to put up with, working on the force.

"Just one thing." He saw Brian raise a quizzical brow. "Are you speaking as the chief of detectives, or as my new stepfather?"

Brian was not quick to answer. "Now that you mention it, both," he finally said, then leaned forward, lowering his voice. "And if you don't comply, I'll tell your mother." He punctuated his threat with a grin.

"Message received, loud and clear." For the first time in two days, Frank McIntyre grinned.

"And if you get a chance," Brian added just before his stepson went out the door, "Andrew would like to see you at breakfast tomorrow."

Everyone knew about Andrew Cavanaugh's breakfasts. More food moved from the former chief of police's stove to the table he'd had specially built than the ordinary high-traffic restaurant. The family patriarch welcomed not just his immediate family, but his nieces and nephews and their significant others as well. There was no such thing as too many people at his table and, like the miracle of the loaves and fishes, Andrew never seemed to run out of food no matter how many people turned up at his door.

"If I get the time," Frank answered.

"Make the time," Brian replied. There was no arguing with his tone.

"Is that an order, sir?"

At which point, Brian smiled. "That's just a friendly suggestion. You really wouldn't want to get on the wrong side of Andrew."

It was an empty threat. Even though everyone knew that in his day, Andrew Cavanaugh was a formidable policeman, when it came to matters concerning his family, Andrew always led with his heart. "I'll keep that in mind, sir," Frank promised.

"You do that, Frank. You do that. And don't forget to tell me what you think of this White Bear—once you give her a chance," he added knowingly.

Frank nodded. "Will do."

He still wasn't all that happy as he went back to the cubbyhole that served as the task force's work area. Becoming integrated into the Cavanaugh family was enough of an adjustment without having some outsider suddenly thrust upon him. It was the *last* thing he needed.

At any other time, he thought, pausing in the doorway and quietly observing the newest addition to his task force, he would have welcomed someone who looked like Julianne. The woman was a head-turner, no doubt about that. But he was in charge of the task force and that changed the rules.

He'd never much liked rules, Frank thought with an inward sigh, but there was no arguing the fact that he was bound by them.

Squaring his shoulders, he walked into the room.

Chapter 2

"So, did Riley get you all caught up?" Frank asked as he came up behind Julianne.

Five victims were on the board, five women from essentially two different walks of life who, at first glance, didn't appear to have anything in common. If there was a prayer of solving this case and bringing down the serial killer, each victim would require more than just a glance. More like an examination under a microscope. No way could she have even scratched the surface in the amount of time that he'd been gone.

Was he testing her?

"She gave me a thumbnail sketch of each victim," Julianne answered guardedly, watching his face for an indication of his thoughts. "It's going to take me a while to actually get caught up." She pulled a folder out from the bottom of the pile of files she'd been given and placed it on top. "While I'm at it, you might want to go over Millie Klein."

The name was unfamiliar to him. "Millie Klein?" he repeated.

"The woman found in the Dumpster in Mission Ridge," Julianne elaborated.

She leaned back in her chair as last Tuesday came rushing back at her. The woman, an estate planning lawyer, had been her first dead body. When she closed her eyes, Julianne could still see the grayish, lifeless body half buried in garbage, her bloodshot eyes open wide and reflecting surprise and horror.

"It looks like your guy was off on a field trip when he had a sudden, uncontrollable urge to kill another woman," she speculated.

"That the way you see it?" Frank asked. Crossing his arms before him, he leaned back and perched on a corner of the desk that Riley had cleared off for the Mission Ridge detective.

McIntyre studied her more intently than was warranted, Julianne thought.

Stare all you want, I'm not leaving.

"Right now, yes," she said flatly. "There's no other reason for him to have strayed from his home ground. Plenty of 'game' for him right here." She'd already gotten a list of clients that Millie had seen that week she was murdered, but so far, everyone had checked out. And every one of them lived in Mission Ridge.

"Maybe it's not the serial killer." He studied her face to see if she was open to the idea—and caught himself thinking she had the most magnificent cheekbones he'd ever seen. "People have been found in Dumpsters before this serial killer started his spree."

"Not in Mission Ridge," she informed him. "We don't have a homicide division in Mission Ridge. Stealing more than one lawn gnome is considered a major crime spree. It's a very peaceful place," she concluded.

Frank's eyes narrowed. He'd been laboring under a basic misunderstanding. "Then you're not a homicide detective?"

"I'm an all-around detective," she answered succinctly. Then, in case he had his doubts and was already labeling her a hick on top of what he probably perceived as her other shortcomings, she was quick to assure him, "Don't worry, I won't get in your way."

It didn't make any sense. Why would they send over someone with no experience? And why had Brian agreed to this? "If you don't mind my asking, why were you sent here?"

That, at least, was an easy enough question to answer. "Because Captain Randolph isn't the kind of man who sweeps things under the rug, or just lets other people do his work for him. This is kind of personal."

Riley walked by just then and without breaking her stride, or saying a word to her brother, dropped off one of the two cans of soda she'd just gotten from the vending machine, placing it on Julianne's desk. Julianne smiled her thanks as she continued.

"Millie Klein was the granddaughter of a friend of his, and he wants justice for his friend. That means seeing her killer pay for her murder. You have the superior department," she informed him without any fanfare. "It just made sense for him to send the case file over here as well as someone with it."

Okay, he'd buy that. But he had another question. "Why you?" She'd just admitted to not having experience and from the looks of her, she couldn't have been a detective *that* long. They had to have someone over at Mission Ridge with more seniority than this lagoon-blue-eyed woman.

Julianne studied him for a long moment before she said anything. "Is your problem with me personal or professional?"

"I don't know you personally."

And he knew better than to think that just because the woman was beautiful she'd gotten ahead on her looks. If he would have so much as hinted at something like that, his sisters—along with all the female members of the Cavanaugh family—would have vivisected him.

So he was saying that his beef with her was professional? She took just as much offense at that as she would have had he said it was personal.

"Professionally, I worked my tail off to get to where I am." Her eyes darkened, turning almost a cobalt blue. "And you don't need to know me personally not to like me 'personally.'" She set her jaw hard. "I've run into that all my life."

Prejudice was something he'd been raised to fight against and despise. "Because you're Native American," he assumed.

"You don't have to be politically correct," she told him. "*Indian* will do fine." The term had never bothered her, or any of the other people she'd grown up with. She didn't see it as an insult. "Or *Navajo* if you want to be more specific."

"Navajo," Frank repeated with a nod. He'd bet his badge that there was more than just Navajo to her. Those blue eyes of hers didn't just come by special delivery. "And you won't find that here," he informed her.

"Other Navajos?"

"No, prejudice because you happen to be something someone else isn't. I don't care if you're a Native American—"

"Indian," she corrected.

"Indian," he repeated. "What I don't like is not having a say in who works for me." But even that could be remedied. "But you prove to me that you can pull your weight, and we'll get along fine."

That sounded fair enough. "Consider it pulled," Julianne told him.

With that out of the way, he nodded at her desk. "I'll look at that folder you brought now."

Julianne held the folder out to him. It was thin compared to the ones that Riley had given her. There was a folder complied with random notes and information on each victim posted on the board.

"You know, all that information was input on the computer," he told her. He indicated the small notebook computer Riley had managed to mysteriously produce for the new detective. It had to have come from one of the other squad rooms, but he wasn't about to ask which one. This was a case where "Don't ask, don't tell" applied particularly nicely. "You can access it easily enough."

Rather than draw the notebook to her, she moved the folders closer. "I like the feel of paper," Julianne told him. "If the electricity goes down, the paper is still here."

Frank laughed shortly. He didn't hear that very often, and never from anyone under thirty. "Old-fashioned?" he guessed.

She'd never thought of herself in those terms, going out of her way not to have anything to do with the old ways to which grandmother had clung.

"I prefer to say that I like the tried and true." With that, she lowered her eyes and got back to her reading.

Frank knew when to leave well enough alone.

Julianne was still going through the files and rereading pertinent parts at the end of the day, making notes to herself as she went along.

She did her best to remain divorced from the victims, from feeling anything as she reviewed descriptions of the crime scenes. She deliberately glossed over the photographs included in each file.

The photographs posted on the board showed off each victim at what could be described as her best, before the world—or the killer—had gotten to her. The photographs in the files were postmortem shots of the women. Julianne made a point of flipping the photographs over rather than attempting to study them.

"Pretty gruesome, aren't they?" Riley commented.

Julianne looked up, surprised to find Riley standing in front of her desk. She'd gotten absorbed in the last folder, Polly Barker, a single mother who made ends meet by turning tricks. Her three-year-old daughter,

Donna, had been taken by social services the day after the woman's body was discovered. Despite her best efforts, Julianne's heart ached, not for the mother, but for the child the woman had left behind.

She closed the folder now. "Yes."

"I don't blame you for not wanting to look at them, but I really think you should."

Julianne glanced at Riley, somewhat surprised though she made sure not to show it. She'd sensed that the other woman was watching her, but more out curiosity than a of desire to assess the way she worked.

"Why? I've got all the details right there in the files." She nodded at the stack.

"You're supposed to be the fresh pair of eyes," Riley reminded her. "Maybe you'll see something we didn't."

Taking a deep breath, Julianne flipped over the set of photographs she'd just set aside. It wasn't that she was squeamish, just that there was something so hopeless about the dead women's faces. She'd fought against hopelessness all of her life and if given the choice, she would have rather avoided the photographs taken at the crime scene.

But Riley was right. She *was* supposed to be the fresh set of eyes and although she doubted she would see something the others had missed, stranger things had happened.

The first thing she saw was a tiny cross carved into the victim's shoulder.

Just as there had been on Millie's.

In his own twisted mind, was the killer sending his victims off to their maker marked for redemption? Was he some kind of religious zealot, or just messing with the collective mind of the people trying to capture him?

After a beat, she raised her eyes to Riley's. "How long?"

Riley looked at her, confused. "How long what?"

Julianne moved the photographs away without looking down. "How long before you stopped seeing their lifeless faces in your sleep?"

Riley nodded. She knew exactly what the woman meant. "I'll let you know when it happens," Riley told her. And then she smiled. "The trick is to fill your life up so that there's no time to think about them that way. And to find the killer," she added with feeling, "so that they—and you—can rest in peace." Riley glanced at her watch. It was after five. "Shift's over. Would you like to go and get a drink?"

While she appreciated the offer, getting a drink held no allure for her. Her father had been an alcoholic, dead before his time. Her uncle, Mary's father, while not an alcoholic, was a mean drunk when he did imbibe.

Julianne shook her head. "I don't drink."

"Doesn't have to be alcohol," Riley told her. "They serve ginger ale there. And coffee." It was obvious that she wasn't going to take no for an answer easily. "I just think you need to unwind a little. And it wouldn't hurt to mingle," she added. "Might make the rest of this experience tolerable for you."

What would make the experience tolerable would be finally finding Mary, but, having kept everything to herself for most of her life, she wasn't ready to share that just yet. For a moment, Julianne debated her answer. Turning Riley down would make her seem standoffish and she didn't want to generate any hard feelings beyond the ones Frank seemed to be harboring.

"All right." She rose, closing her desk drawer. "I'll follow you."

"Great." Riley grinned, moving over to her desk to grab her purse. "I'll drive slow."

"No need. I can keep up," Julianne told her.

Riley nodded. "I bet you can."

Rafferty's was more a tavern than an actual bar. While it was true that on most nights, members of the Aurora police force went there to unwind and shed some of their more haunting demons before going home to their families, the establishment just as readily welcomed spouses and their children. In many cases it was a home away from home for detectives and patrol officers alike.

And Rafferty's was also where, on any given evening, at least several members of the Cavanaugh family could be found.

This particular evening there were more than a few Cavanaughs in the bar and Riley made a point of introducing Julianne to all of them, as well as her older brother, Zack.

"Taylor's probably out on a date," Riley told her matter-of-factly, carrying a mug of beer and an individual bottle of ginger ale over to the small table she'd staked out for the two of them as soon as they'd walked in.

Julianne took a seat, accepting the ginger ale. Riley had refused to let her pay. "Taylor?"

"My sister." Riley sat down opposite her. "She's the social butterfly of the family. Like Frank," she tagged on as an afterthought. "Or he was until he got assigned to this case."

After having met the man, it was hard for Julianne to picture Frank McIntyre as anything but solemn. Except for that one instance, he hadn't smiled during the course of the day, not even when the smaller of the two detectives, Sanchez, had made a joke.

Keeping her observation to herself, Julianne scanned the crowded room. As she recognized faces, it struck her that she'd been introduced to more people than she'd realized.

"And you're related to these people?" she asked Riley, slightly in awe as the fact sank in.

Riley nodded, taking a sip of her beer before answering. "Through marriage," she qualified, although she'd gotten to know a great many of them from day-to-day interaction ever since she joined the police force. "My mother is married to the chief of detectives, Brian Cavanaugh. Real good guy," she said with a wide, approving smile. Brian was the man her mother was meant to have married. He treated her far better than the man who had fathered all four of her children. Brian Cavanaugh was the man she herself had always pretended was her father, when times became rocky. "They used to be partners back when they were on patrol."

Julianne looked at her in surprise. "Your mother was on the job, too?" This police department really *was* a family affair, she thought. It made her feel even more of an outsider than usual.

"Yes. Almost everyone I know is on the job," Riley told her.

It was on the tip of Riley's tongue to mention her late

father, but since his career ended in disgrace, she decided not to go into something she didn't really want to talk about. Besides, if Julianne remained on the task force long enough, she was pretty sure the woman would hear about it from one source or another. Facts had come to light not all that long ago about how her father had faked his own death and bided his time to come back for the money he'd stolen from drug runners. That wasn't something to discuss with a stranger.

"My father made her quit the force after she was shot—"

"Shot?" Julianne echoed.

Riley nodded. The story was so much a part of her life, sometimes she forgot that not everyone knew about it. "While on the job. Brian saved her. Stopped the blood with his own hands and all but willed the life back into her as he waited for the paramedics."

"I can see why your father wanted her to quit."

He had pressured her mother to leave the force because he was jealous of Brian, not because he feared for her life, but Riley kept that to herself as well.

"Being off the force didn't suit her. Being a law-enforcement officer was in her blood so, once Frank was in high school, she got back into it. To keep peace in the family, she took a desk job, but she figured that was better than nothing." She took another sip, then added, "I guess you just can't keep a good cop down."

Julianne heard the pride in Riley McIntyre's voice and a trace of envy surfaced.

What was that like, she wondered, being proud of your parents? Of what they'd done and were doing, and the effect all that had on the lives of other people? She would have given *anything* to experience that.

But there was no sense in wishing. Those weren't the cards that fate had dealt her and she'd already made her peace with that years back.

There'd been no other choice, really, except maybe to wind up the way her father had. But she absolutely refused to go down that road and let that happen. Pride wouldn't allow her to.

"How's it going?"

The deep, baritone voice asking the question came from behind her. Rather certain the question wasn't directed at her, Julianne still turned around in her chair to see who was doing the asking. She found herself looking up at yet another law-enforcement officer. He wasn't in uniform, but there was just an air about that man that fairly shouted: authority. He was older and had a kind, intelligent face, not to mention a handsome one. He also had the ability to take over a room the moment he entered.

She guessed his identity a second before he told her.

Smiling, Brian extended his hand to her. "Brian Cavanaugh," he said easily, as if he was just another cop on the force rather than the chief of detectives. Julianne started to get up out of respect for the man and his rank, but he waved her back into her seat. "No need for that," he told her. "I stopped by the task force and Sanchez told me that Riley was bringing you here for a quick orientation session," he laughed.

His deep blue eyes scanned the room quickly. "They're a bit overwhelming at first," he agreed. "But they grow on you." He turned his eyes on her again. "Glad to have you aboard for the ride."

Something about the man made her feel comfortable. As much as she was able to be.

"Glad someone is." The words came out before she could tamp them down. Living off the reservation had made her lax, she upbraided herself.

"Don't let Frank get to you," Riley said. "He's channeled all his usual enthusiasm into solving the case and I know he can come on strong sometimes, but there's the heart of a puppy underneath," she guaranteed. Turning around, she saw the door opening. "Speak of the devil."

"Riley," Brian laughed, "that's no way to talk about your brother."

"No offense, Brian, but you don't know him like I do." And then she winked at Julianne, as if they shared a secret.

Julianne wondered what it meant. Before she could make a comment or frame a question, she saw that Frank was crossing the room.

And coming straight toward them.

All her natural defenses instantly rose.

Chapter 3

Riley dramatically placed her hand to her chest, like a heroine in a 1950s melodrama, feigning shock.

"I didn't think I'd see you here, mingling with the masses," she said to her brother as Frank approached their table.

Frank spared her a slight, reproving frown. He was bone tired and desperately in need of unwinding. "Give it a rest, Riley. This is after hours."

Stealing an empty chair from the next table, he pulled it over to the one occupied by his sister and Julianne. He straddled the chair and folded his arms over the back.

Raising his hand, he made eye contact with the bartender and nodded. The barkeep took a mug and filled it with beer on tap and handed it to the lone waitress working the floor. Only then did Frank look at the detective from Mission Ridge and ask, "Mind if I join you?"

"No, I don't mind," she answered crisply. "I was on my way out, anyway." Rising from her chair, she nodded at Riley. "Thanks for the ginger ale and the introductions."

"Don't mention it," Riley replied, doing her best to hide her amusement.

"I'll walk you out," Brian volunteered, then told his stepchildren, "I promised your mother I'd be home early tonight. I just wanted to stop by and see how the new detective was doing." And then he smiled at Julianne. "From the looks of it, I'd say she's doing just fine."

Not accustomed to compliments, Julianne murmured a barely audible, "Thanks," before turning on her heel and heading for the front door.

Brian was right beside her.

"Well, that's a first," Riley said the moment she judged that Julianne was out of earshot. She looked at her brother with no small amazement. "I don't think I ever saw a woman go out of her way to get away from you before."

Frank handed the waitress a five and then picked up the mug she'd placed on the table in front of him. He shrugged, dismissing the incident. "She said she was leaving anyway."

"She only said that *after* you sat down," Riley pointed out. The waitress cleared away Julianne's ginger ale and made her way back to the bar. "Face it, Frank, you're losing your charm."

Frank eyed his sister over the rim of his mug. "I'm also losing my patience with smart-alecky sisters." He took a long sip, then added, "If you weren't so damn good at your job, Riley, I'd have you taken off the task force."

To which Riley merely shook her head, as if at a loss whether to pity him or hand his head to him. "Careful, Frank, this job is turning you sour." And then she leaned in, her expression becoming more serious. "Really, Frank, lighten up a little. You're trying too damn hard."

They had a difference of opinion there. He'd had the case for over a month and in that time, they'd compiled nothing but data. Data and no viable suspects. And he had an uneasy feeling they were running out of time.

"Way I see it, I'm not trying hard enough." His expression turned grim. "The killer's still out there somewhere, daring us to catch him. Every second he's out there is a second less the next victim has."

"We'll get him," Riley said confidently. "*You'll* get him," she emphasized. It wasn't often that she told him she thought he was good. But he was. "Just don't alienate everyone else while you're doing it."

Rising, he turned his chair around so that he could sit in it properly. He sighed and picked up the mug again. Another long sip didn't change anything. "Sometimes I think I'm in over my head."

"We all are." Riley laughed shortly. "This is where the dog paddle comes in *really* handy. We're all just treading water until the killer makes a mistake. When he does, we've got him."

The shrug was careless. He didn't know if he bought into that philosophy. So far, the killer had been anything but careless. It was as if he was a ghost, depositing lifeless bodies into Dumpsters. Six in all, counting the one in Mission Ridge, and *nobody* had seen him.

To get his mind off the case, Frank changed the subject. "So, did you learn anything about the detective from Mission Ridge?" he asked, doing his best to sound offhanded.

Riley slanted a glance at her brother's face. There was interest there, she'd bet a month's pay on it. Personal probably although he'd try to keep it professional.

"Not a thing, except that she's thorough." The woman had studied the files without getting up from her desk all afternoon. "But she's not exactly chatty."

"Yeah, well, that might be a nice change," he speculated, looking at her deliberately.

Riley swatted him.

"Hey," he warned, pulling his head back. "You're not supposed to hit your superior."

"We're off duty, remember?" Riley countered. "You've got to learn how to turn it off, little brother, or it'll take you apart."

Frank said nothing to confirm or deny the wisdom of her words. Instead, he just took another sip of his beer and thought about the woman fate—and his stepfather—had brought into his life.

Julianne could have driven back home. "Home" was only about forty-two miles away. But in the interest of time, Julianne had decided to rent a room in a hotel close to the police headquarters.

Taking the suitcase she'd thrown together last night out of the trunk of her car, she walked into the Aurora

Hotel, a wide, three-story building that, from the outside, resembled one of those 24/7 gyms that had become the rage.

The decor inside could have used a little modernizing and upgrading. But in comparison to what she'd lived with when she was growing up, it was on par with the Taj Mahal.

The lobby was empty. No one sat in the five chairs scattered about, their gray color all but fading into the equally gray rug. The bored, sleepy-eyed desk clerk came to life as she approached the front desk, obviously grateful for any diversion that would make this long, drawn-out evening move a little faster to its conclusion.

Ten minutes later, with her keycard in her hand, Julianne got out on the third floor and walked to her room. As uninspired as the lobby, it at least gave the semblance of cleanliness, which was all she required. Setting her suitcase down by the pressboard writing desk, she didn't bother unpacking. There was time enough for that later.

Right now, she had a job to do, which was the real reason she hadn't balked at being loaned out to an adjacent police department. She had streets to drive up and down, people to question and show the picture she carried with her at all times.

Throwing some water into her face, Julianne was ready. Dinner would be fast food. She didn't care what; it was just fuel anyway.

She wasn't one to believe in miracles, but, as she'd said to Riley, she liked to think that she had an open mind about things. Silently, she challenged God to prove her wrong about miracles. Someone had told her that finding Mary would come under the heading of a miracle.

Mary.

Her cousin was out there somewhere because living on the street was preferable to living at home, subjected to nightly abuse at the hands of a father who didn't deserve the name. "Monster" would have been a far more fitting title.

But he would never bother anyone again. Events had arranged themselves so that she could make that claim to Mary—when she found her—with certainty.

She hadn't gone over to her uncle's house to kill him even though she'd wished the man dead more than once. But when he'd come at her the way she knew in her heart that he had come at Mary time and again, she'd had no choice but to defend herself any way she could.

Julianne wasn't even sure just how the knife had come into her hand. She only knew that when she'd told him she'd use it if he didn't back off, her uncle had laughed at her. He'd mocked her, saying that she was just as cowardly as her father had been.

And then he'd told her what he'd do to her for daring to point the knife at him. She remembered her blood running cold. Remembered feeling almost paralyzing guilt for not having taken Mary with her before her cousin had been forced to run away.

Her uncle had lunged at her, knocking the knife from her hand and screaming obscenities at her. There'd been a struggle for possession of the weapon. They'd wrestled and though to this day she wasn't certain how it happened, somehow the blade had wound up in his chest—up to the hilt.

Her first inclination had been to run. But she knew she could never outrun her own conscience, so she'd gone in to the captain without bothering to change her torn clothing. Numb, in shock, she'd told him the whole story.

People who lived in the vicinity knew the kind of man her uncle had been. In short order, Harry White Bear's death was ruled self-defense, and she was free to go on with her life.

Her search for Mary began that day.

She wanted to bring her cousin home with her, the way she should have done right from the beginning instead of fleeing herself and leaving Mary behind. She'd left because her uncle had made advances, but she'd never, in her wildest dreams, thought that he would force himself on his own daughter.

That was when she still believed that there was some good in everyone.

She didn't believe that anymore.

Julianne wanted to find Mary to let her know that she didn't have to look over her shoulder anymore, that her father wasn't going to hurt her again, that she could become something other than a woman who lived on the streets.

"I'm going to make it up to you, Mary. Somehow, someway, I'm going to make it up to you," she murmured to the photograph she'd placed face up on the passenger seat. "But first, I've got to find you."

Julianne knew she had a long night ahead of her. It didn't matter. All that mattered was finding Mary.

* * *

The next morning, after only about four hours of sleep, Julianne was at her desk by seven-thirty. She wanted to go over the last of the files she hadn't gotten to the previous day.

When she heard someone entering the squad room shortly after she arrived, Julianne was surprised. From what she'd been told, the detectives came in at eight-thirty. She'd assumed that she'd have some time to herself before the room filled up with noise.

Her surprise doubled when she looked up and found Frank standing over her desk. Something instantly tightened inside of her. Every nerve ending had inexplicably gone on high alert and she wasn't completely sure why.

"Can I help you?" she asked, successfully stripping her voice of all emotion and the tension.

He studied her for a moment before asking, "Whose picture were you showing around on McFadden last night, White Bear?"

The question caught her utterly off guard. Stunned, Julianne couldn't answer him immediately. How had he known where she was last night? Was he following her? That had to be it, but why?

A sudden thrust of anger surged through her. This wasn't going to work. She wanted out. Her eyes narrowed. "You were spying on me?"

He heard the accusation in her voice, but managed not to rise to the bait. While she was part of his task force, he was accountable for her. He needed to know exactly what he was getting himself into. "I was driving down McFadden when I saw you."

Julianne pressed her lips together, trying to choose her words carefully. She had a temper, but most of the time managed to bury it. Now it was closer to the surface than usual. She wasn't sure she believed him, and yet, what sense did it make for him to be spying on her?

For now, she gave him the benefit of the doubt—as long as he could answer her question to her satisfaction. "What were you doing there?"

How had this gotten turned around to be about him? Still, he'd learned that in order to get something, you had to give something. So rather than pull rank, which he was obviously entitled to do, he answered her question.

"I was retracing what I thought might have been the last victim's steps. What were *you* doing there?"

He waited to see what kind of an answer she'd give him. It didn't seem plausible that she would be out, her first night on the case—her first night in Aurora—showing around one of the victim's photographs to the ladies of the evening on that particular corner of the world.

She hated being accountable to anyone. It had taken her a while before she could trust Captain Randolph and follow instructions. This was not going to be easy. But she owed it to Randolph to try. The man had put his reputation on the line and taken her side during the investigation into her uncle's death.

"Asking questions," she replied tersely.

His eyes never left hers. It impressed him that she didn't flinch or look away. "Isn't that a little in the overachiever range?"

She shrugged carelessly. "The sooner this case gets

solved, the sooner I can go back to Mission Ridge—and get out of your hair."

"Very noble of you," he commented. She wasn't sure she detected a note of sarcasm in his voice. And then he pressed, "So that's all you were doing? Showing one of the victim's photographs around?"

She raised her chin, silently daring him to disprove her. "Yes."

His eyes pinned her. "Which one?"

Julianne blinked, her mind scrambling for a name. She stalled for time. "Excuse me?"

"Which victim?" he asked. "Which victim's picture were you showing around? Seems like a simple enough question." The longer she didn't give him an answer, the less he believed her.

Damn him. She didn't like being cornered. It took Julianne only half a beat to make a selection. He wouldn't know the difference. Not unless he'd gotten out of the car and questioned the hookers she'd talked to after she was gone. And even then, he wouldn't get an answer. Some of them seemed pretty out of it.

"That one." Julianne pointed to the photograph of a somewhat bedraggled woman whose picture was heading up the third column.

He turned to look, then approached the bulletin board. "That's Andrea Katz. She was a computer programmer for Dulles and Edwards." He looked back at Julianne. "Why would you be asking around about her there? Andrea Katz wasn't found anywhere near that part of town."

Why was he pushing this? "Okay, so it was the one next to her."

Again, he turned just to verify what he already knew. He'd gone over and over this board time and again, searching for the one connection he needed. The women's likenesses were all embossed in his brain.

"Ramona Hernandez. Hooker. Found in a Dumpster behind a diner in the older part of the city," he recited. "Want to try again?" he asked cheerfully.

It was getting harder and harder to hang on to her temper. "What do you want from me, McIntyre?"

"The truth, White Bear. I'd like the truth. Is that too much to ask?"

He was crowding her space. She was a very, very private person, one who had trouble filling out anything beyond her name on a form, feeling that it was her business, not anyone else's. But what harm would telling him do, Julianne silently argued with herself. And if it would get him off her back, maybe telling him would be worth it.

"Okay," she bit off the word. "In my off hours, I thought I'd try to find my cousin, Mary. Mary White Bear. She's a runaway. Just before I left Mission Ridge, someone told me that they thought they saw her in Aurora." Again Julianne lifted her chin pugnaciously. He'd agitated her and part of her was almost spoiling for a fight. "Satisfied?"

Questions about the woman before him began materializing in Frank's head at a prodigious rate. "No."

Her eyes narrowed into annoyed slits. "Well, there's nothing I can do about that, is there?"

Now there they had a difference of opinion. He allowed a smile to curve his mouth. "You could tell me why you thought you had to lie about that and keep it to yourself."

She hadn't told Randolph about Mary and she got along with the Captain fairly well. Julianne couldn't see herself voluntarily sharing something so personal with a stranger. She shrugged carelessly, combing her fingers through her hair and sending it back over her shoulder. She said the first thing that came to mind. "I figured you wouldn't want me distracted."

"I don't," he agreed firmly. "But what you do in your time away from the job is none of my business." And then, because there was an aura of danger about this woman he needed to find out more about, he qualified his statement. "Unless you wind up killing someone."

Julianne looked at him sharply, adrenaline rushing through her veins. Had he looked into her background? Did he know about her uncle?

Frank saw the heightened awareness, saw the wary look that entered her eyes. White Bear, he realized, just might be capable of anything. If she turned out to be a loose cannon, he wanted her off his task force. "*Did* you wind up killing someone last night?"

"No."

Well, that was a relief. But he was still going to keep an eye on her. Ordinarily, that wouldn't have been a hardship. But her looks were distracting and he couldn't afford to be distracted, not until the killer was caught and this case was closed.

"Okay then, I've got no problem with you looking for your cousin during your downtime." Turning away from her, he began to walk toward the cubicle that served as his office. "Can I see it?"

"See what?" she asked warily.

This woman trusted no one, he thought, as more questions about her came to mind—the first being why was she so distrustful? "The photograph you were showing around. Maybe I've seen her," he added when she made no effort to retrieve the photograph from her purse.

Maybe he had, Julianne thought.

No stone unturned, remember?

She was going to have to do something about her defensiveness, Julianne silently upbraided herself, taking her purse out of the desk's bottom drawer. Opening it, she pulled out the photograph of her cousin and held it up to him.

The girl in the photograph looked like a younger version of Julianne. She had incredibly sad eyes. "Pretty girl," he commented.

"She would have been better off if she wasn't," Julianne answered grimly, looking at the photograph herself.

"Meaning?"

Julianne raised her eyes to his. "Meaning that she looked a lot like my dead aunt. And the first one who noticed was my uncle."

Her tone of voice had Frank quickly reading between the lines. Incest was a crime he could never quite wrap his head around. It was just too heinous. "So she ran away from home before he—"

"No," Julianne contradicted angrily, "she ran away from home *after* he…"

She deliberately let her voice trail off without finishing the sentence, but there was no mistaking her meaning.

Frank took a breath. Maybe that was why this woman was so angry. It would have certainly made him angry to have a cousin of his violated by the very person who was supposed to protect her.

"Sorry to hear that," he said, his voice as full of feeling as hers was monotone.

She thought he honestly meant that and it made her regret the tone she'd taken with him. When she reached for the photograph he was still holding, he didn't surrender it immediately.

"Why don't I have copies made of this?" Frank suggested. "Pass it around to the beat cops. Maybe one of them will see her and get back to us."

Us. It was on the tip of her tongue to say that she hadn't asked for his help, but she swallowed the words. She had to start trusting someone somewhere along the line or she was just going to wind up self-destructing. That wasn't going to help Mary at all.

Julianne pressed her lips together. Time to take the hand that was reaching out to her, she silently ordered. Taking it didn't automatically make her weak.

"That would be good, yes," she agreed.

But just as he began to head for the copy machine, the phone on Riley's desk rang. Since he was closer to it than Julianne was, Frank picked it up.

"McIntyre."

Julianne saw his face darken as he listened. His eyes went flat.

"We'll be right there," he said grimly before hanging up. "C'mon," he told her, putting the photograph down on her desk. For now, it was going to have to wait. "They just found another body."

Chapter 4

The Dumpster was clear across town behind a popular restaurant that served Chinese cuisine, buffet style.

Gin-Ling's was a popular food source for the homeless. Confronted with the all-you-can-eat philosophy, more than half the patrons who came to Gin-Ling's had a tendency to overload their plates. Discovering that their stomachs weren't really as large as they'd surmised usually followed shortly thereafter. Since the restaurant didn't provide doggie bags, most people left the uneaten portions on their plates.

Most evenings, the twin Dumpsters behind Gin-Ling's were filled to overflowing.

This time, one of them was more "overflowing" than the other.

Parking his Crown Victoria sedan at the end of the

alley bordering the crime scene, Frank got out. As he began to make his way to the Dumpster where the newest gruesome discovery had been made by a homeless man with, it turned out, a very weak stomach, he pulled a pair of rubber gloves out of his pocket and started to put them on.

Mentally, Frank wished he had coveralls on instead of the suit he was wearing. But when he'd dressed this morning, he hadn't been planning on undertaking a safari through a Dumpster.

Just before he reached the Dumpster under scrutiny, Frank glanced toward Julianne and saw that she was putting on her own pair of plastic gloves. He noted that her mouth was set grimly and recalled what Riley had told him last night. The detective from Mission Ridge wasn't used to homicides.

"You up to this?" he asked her suddenly.

Busy taking in everything around her, significant or otherwise, it took Julianne a second to realize that McIntyre was talking to her.

"Excuse me?"

He stopped walking. "Riley said that you mentioned that the woman who was killed in Mission Ridge was your first dead body." These things could be pretty unsettling and he didn't want to be sidetracked by a detective throwing up her breakfast.

Julianne wasn't sure where the detective was going with this, only that she probably wasn't going to like it. "So?"

"So," he continued patiently, "if you'd rather sit this

out—until at least the rest of the team gets here—I understand."

Right. He understood. And then he'd use that against her to send her back. She didn't need those kinds of favors. She was here and she planned to remain here until she found Mary and, oh yes, helped to find the serial killer as well.

"Thank you but there's no need to worry about me," she told him coolly. "And Millie Klein wasn't my first dead body," she informed him. "Just my first homicide."

Her uncle had been the first dead person she'd seen. And that scene had been made that much more brutal because he was dead by her hand. Blood had been everywhere. She could still see him staring down at the knife, anger and shock on his face as the life force fled from his veins.

But there was no way she was about to go into that now.

Frank could sense she was holding something back. He had a feeling that if she were drowning, White Bear'd throw the life preserver back at his head, determined to save herself on her own. Pride was a good thing, but there was such a thing as too much of it. For the time being, he let it go.

"Okay."

As he approached the Dumpster, he saw that the crime scene investigators had already been called in. A slight, younger man was busy snapping photographs of the area directly surrounding the one Dumpster, while another man, older and heavyset, was inside the Dumpster. Wrinkling his nose involuntarily against the pungent smell, he was taking close-ups of a woman who could no longer protest.

Overturning a wooden crate that, if the image painted on the side was correct, had once contained bean sprouts, Frank pushed the box next to the Dumpster and used it as a step to facilitate his getting into the Dumpster. The thought of just diving in seemed somehow repugnant.

The smell of death and rotting food assaulted him. Still, a job was a job. The first thing he noticed, before he climbed in, was the wig. A blond wig, obviously belonging to the victim, had slipped halfway off her head.

The second thing he noticed was the woman's face.

He'd seen that face before. Less than an hour ago.

Stunned at the way fate sometimes toyed with them, he turned to see that Julianne was gamely about to follow suit, waiting her turn to use the wooden crate as a stepstool.

"Stay back," he ordered.

The barked commanded caught her off guard. "Why? I said I can handle it."

Not this. "I don't think so," he told her tersely. There was no arguing with his tone.

Except that she refused to be browbeaten. Nor would she accept any special treatment that he could later hold over her head.

"Why don't you let me decide that?" It was a rhetorical question and she didn't wait for an answer. Bracing her hands on the front of the Dumpster, she was about to vault in.

"Might get crowded in here," the investigator speculated.

"White Bear, I said get back," Frank ordered angrily.

He shifted, trying to block her view, but it was too late. Because that was when Julianne saw her. Saw the face of the serial killer's latest victim.

She could almost feel the blood draining out of her face. "Mary."

Frank jumped down from his perch in time to catch her as her knees gave out.

Julianne vaguely felt arms closing around her even as fire and ice passed over her body. For a split second, the world threatened to disappear into the black abyss that mushroomed out all around her.

Only the steeliest of resolves enabled her to fight back against the darkness, against the overwhelming nausea that almost succeeded in bringing up her hastily consumed dinner from last night.

Sucking in air, Julianne struggled against the strong arms that held her prisoner.

"I'm all right," she insisted, hot anger mingling with hot tears she damned herself for shedding. "I'm all right," she repeated, almost shouting the words at Frank.

The sound of an approaching car had Frank looking down the alley. He recognized Riley's vehicle. "Look, why don't I have Riley take you back?" he suggested kindly.

She bristled at what she thought was pity. "No." The word tore from her throat like a war cry. Shrugging out of Frank's hold, willing her legs to stiffen, Julianne moved back to the Dumpster. "I'm not going anywhere," she cried defiantly.

"You're off the case, White Bear," he told her tersely.

Her head snapped around and she glared at him. "No, I'm not," she insisted. "You can't do that."

Oh, but he could. And he had to. "You're related to the victim."

Her eyes blazed and she took out all the pain she was feeling on him. "You wouldn't have known that if you hadn't invaded my privacy."

He wasn't going to get sucked into nitpicking. "Doesn't change anything. You can't—"

Suddenly grabbing his arm, Julianne dragged him over to the side, away from the investigator who had made no secret of listening to the exchange. It killed her to beg, but if she had to, she would.

"Please, I'm asking you not to take me off the case. That girl in the Dumpster is the only family I have. I had," she corrected. Even as she said it, she could feel her heart twisting in her chest. *I'm sorry, Mary. I'm so sorry.* "She's in there because of me."

"How do you figure that?"

"You're not going to be satisfied until I rip myself open in front of you, are you?"

This woman could raise his temper faster than anyone he'd ever encountered, but his aim wasn't to irritate her. He had only one focus. "My only interest is in solving the case. Now if you have anything to contribute that might be helpful—"

The words, propelled by her guilt, rushed out. "If I'd taken her with me instead of leaving her with her father, she wouldn't have run away, wouldn't have tried to support herself by resorting to the world's oldest profession."

He didn't buy that. There was *always* another choice.

"Lots of other ways for a woman to earn a living besides that," he told her.

Julianne knew she would have never resorted to that, but she wasn't Mary. Mary's demons had branded her. "Not if she thinks she's worthless. Her father didn't just steal her innocence, he stole her soul. And I let him." She pointed toward the Dumpster. "That's on me."

His eyes held hers. Frank could all but feel her misery. "You knew what was going on?"

"No, but I should have." If she hadn't been so involved in making a life for herself, she would have realized what was going on, would have understood the desperate look in Mary's eyes.

If there was the slightest case for her staying, he thought, White Bear wasn't going to do either of them any good by blaming herself for something she had no control over.

"Listen, I'm not up on my Navajo culture, but I don't recall hearing that the tribe had a lock on clairvoyance. If you didn't know, you didn't know. What happened to your cousin isn't your fault." But he could see that his words made no impression on her. It was as if they bounced off her head.

He had to let her work the case. He *had* to. "Please don't take me off the case. I've got to find her killer. I owe it to Mary."

"Hey, anything wrong?" Riley called out as she came up to join them. Sanchez and Hill stood directly behind her. Both veered over to the Dumpster that had become Mary's final resting place. Their expressions grim, each detective pulled on a pair of plastic gloves.

Frank saw the unspoken plea in Julianne's eyes as she looked up at him. This was, for the time being, still between the two of them. Being leader sucked, he thought. But there was no way he was about to relinquish the position.

"Turns out White Bear's got a delicate stomach," he told his sister after a pause. "I'm trying to tell her she doesn't have to look at the victim. Plenty to do around here besides staring at a dead woman."

"No shame in that," Riley assured her. "First murder victim I saw, I emptied out my stomach and didn't eat for a week. Frank's right," she continued, placing herself between Julianne and the Dumpster. "There're enough people to document the vic's position and whatnot." She looked at her brother. "Want us to canvas the area?"

The question was a mere formality. She knew procedure as well as Frank. Better probably. But since he was the lead on this, in front of others she'd played along.

"Good a start as any," Frank commented.

He turned back to the Dumpster, intent on doing his own examination of the immediate area as well as getting as concise an overview of the victim as possible.

As he crossed back to the Dumpster, he saw Sanchez stand up and look at him over the side. It was obvious by his grimace that this was *not* the other detective's favorite place to be.

"There's no ID on the vic from what I can see, Frank," Sanchez called out.

"We've got an ID," Frank informed him. "Her name was Mary."

"Mary?" Hill echoed. The older detective clambered

out of the Dumpster. He was less than graceful. "Mary what?" he asked, trying to brush some of the debris off his clothing.

"For now, just Mary," Frank said.

Tagging the victim White Bear would bring immediate focus on the Mission Ridge detective in exactly the fashion she didn't want. He hadn't made up his mind about her. And, he had to admit to himself, in all honesty, he sympathized with what she had to be feeling.

Behind them, the coroner's vehicle pulled up at the mouth of the alley, ready to take victim number seven to the morgue.

Frank turned to glance in Julianne's direction. He saw her looking at him. Very deliberately, she mouthed, "Thank you," before turning away and following Riley to the front of the restaurant.

Don't thank me yet, White Bear, he thought.

Julianne caught a ride back to the precinct with Riley rather than Frank even though she'd initially arrived with him. She was grateful that Riley didn't press her to talk, respecting the fact that she needed some time to process what had happened. She was sure Riley just believed she was traumatized about seeing a murder victim.

Eventually, she had to tell the woman that the serial killer's latest victim was her cousin. Right now, she couldn't bring herself to talk about it. Or Mary. She needed to pull herself together and focus. One thing she knew: She wasn't going home until Mary's killer was caught.

By the time she walked into the room the task force had taken over and made their own, there were two bulletin boards in the room instead of one. Mary's photograph was pinned to the new board. Rather than the unsettling crime-scene photographs, Frank had used the one that she'd brought with her. The one she'd used to show the prostitutes last night.

If only one of them had remembered seeing Mary, maybe she could have gotten to her before …

She was going to drive herself crazy, Julianne silently reprimanded. She had to deal with what *was,* not with what might have been.

It almost hurt her to look at Mary's photograph. Despite the sad eyes, Mary was smiling in the photograph. She had been so young, so pretty. The whole world could have been at her feet had she been allowed to grow up like any normal girl.

It wasn't fair, Julianne thought angrily. It just wasn't fair.

Like someone in a trance, she walked up to the second bulletin board because the one they had had grown too crowded to handle any more victims. Right now, Mary's photograph was the only one on it.

How long would that last?

In the middle of saying something to Hill, Frank abruptly stopped and crossed over to her. "I need you to fill me in on things."

She was grateful that McIntyre was letting her stay, but a wariness crept over her nonetheless. "What things?" she asked.

Because her connection was going to be kept private for the time being, he lowered his voice. "You said she was your only family."

"Yes?" The single word inferred that he had heard correctly.

Same confounding pattern, he thought. "Then she had no brothers or sisters, nobody to ask after her, except for you?"

Where was he going with this? She didn't like moving blindly into something. "Right."

"Just like the others," Frank murmured under his breath, looking at the first bulletin board.

"The others?" She'd read through all the files, but didn't recall seeing that each woman was an only child. Was he referring to something else?

"The other victims," Frank clarified. "That's the only thing they had in common." He looked from one photograph to another, thinking what a terrible waste it all was. "None of the women had anyone in their lives to ask after them if they suddenly went missing."

Julianne took offense at his statement. "She had me," she protested.

He pointed out the obvious. "But you didn't know where she was. So you weren't a presence," he said matter-of-factly. "Or a factor. All these other women, they were all single, or divorced."

"Our second victim was a widow," Riley reminded him, walking into the room from the opposite end. She tossed down her purse on her desk, weary beyond reason. She hated coming up against dead ends and that was all their canvassing had yielded: dead ends.

Frank shrugged. "Same difference. For all intents and purposes, they were all alone. No immediate family in the area to ask about them if they suddenly vanished.

Employers assumed they were taking a sick day. And who misses a hooker?" He deliberately avoided looking at Julianne as he posed the question. "A cold trail is harder to follow than a hot one," he concluded.

His eyes swept over the photographs thoughtfully. There *had* to be something else. Something that tied them together. Something they were all missing. But what?

"Maybe he just picks them at random," Hill suggested. That had been his theory all along.

But Frank shook his head. "One or two, maybe. But the chances of all seven of them being loners is astronomical," he insisted. "No, the killer hand selected them."

"Okay, assuming you're right," Julianne said, crossing her arms before her, waiting to be convinced. "Why? Why these particular women and not another group?"

"If we knew that, we could narrow our search, couldn't we?" Frank countered, banking down a wave of sarcasm before it entered his voice.

He looked at her for a long moment, still not certain he was doing the right thing by letting her remain on the task force. Rules dictated that he take her off if she had a personal stake in it and this was really personal.

"I need to talk to you in private," he said abruptly, walking into the hall.

Those were the exact words the principal had used the day he'd called her into his office. He called her in to tell her that her father was found dead. She was eighteen and four days away from graduating high school.

Julianne struggled against the chill that slipped down her spine now as she walked out of the room and followed Frank into the hall.

The moment they were out of earshot of the others, he turned to look at her. "I'm not sure that letting you stay is the right thing to do," he told her honestly. "The rules—"

She didn't let him finish. "You're not someone who goes by the rules."

She said it with such certainty, he was sure Riley had to have tipped her off. "Who told you that?"

"Nobody," she replied quietly. "I can see it in your eyes."

"That Navajo clairvoyance again?" This time he allowed a touch of sarcasm to come through.

"No, that's gut instincts. Cops are supposed to have them," she reminded him. He wasn't coming around, she thought. She needed something more. There was only one card she had left to play. She hoped it would do the trick. "You come from a big family, McIntyre. How would you feel if that was *your* cousin's picture posted on the bulletin board and you thought you let her down? Would you just back away, pack up and go home and let someone else take over finding her killer?" she challenged. "I don't think so."

Frank didn't answer immediately. But he knew how he'd react. He'd track down the bastard and make him pay for what he'd done.

But this wasn't his cousin, it was hers and that made all the difference in the world.

Being leader was a no-win situation, he thought darkly. But, for what it was worth, it did allow him to call the shots—until he wound up shooting himself in the foot, he thought cryptically.

"Okay, you can stay. For now," he qualified. "But that means that you don't go Lone Ranger on me, understand?"

"Wrong character," she corrected with a glimmer of a smile on her lips. "Tonto was the Indian."

"Yeah, but Tonto followed the rules."

She laughed shortly. It was all in how you viewed things, she thought. "Tonto teamed up with a white guy in a mask." That was back in the day when stereotypes were the rule, not the exception. And pairing the two together had gone against type. "There *were* no rules."

"There are here." She couldn't mistake his meaning. There were rules and she was to abide by them.

Julianne took a deep breath. "Duly noted," she said. Mentally holding her breath, she asked, "So, do I get to stay?"

"You get to stay."

"Thank you. Anything else?"

"Not at the moment," he told her.

With a nod of her head, Julianne turned around and walked back to the squad room.

Unconsciously noting the almost infinitesimal sway of her hips as she moved, Frank had an uneasy feeling he was going to live to regret his decision as he followed Julianne back into the squad room.

Chapter 5

"We're going to start from scratch," Frank announced once he walked back into the squad room.

Hill set down the coffee—his twelfth cup of the day—and frowned. "Come again?"

"We're going to question anybody who had any interaction with our victims. The career women," he specified. "Talk to their coworkers, their neighbors, find out what supermarkets they went to and talk to the checkers. Sometimes people share things with strangers they wouldn't tell their friends."

"These people didn't have friends," Sanchez reminded him. "They had stepping-stones. They climbed up on the backs of others," he elaborated, when Julianne gave him a puzzled look.

"Maybe somebody had it in for one of them," Frank theorized.

"And did what, killed all these other women to hide it?" Riley asked, incredulously.

"Maybe he killed the first one for a reason—and discovered that he liked the feeling. Liked being God in that tiny universe," Julianne said, thinking out loud.

Frank nodded, the movement becoming more enthusiastic as he thought over what Julianne was saying. "Good. Go with that. Talk to Andrea Katz's employer, her neighbors, her coworkers, anyone you can find. Get her credit history and see where she shopped, what restaurants she went to, what movie theaters she frequented. Who her boyfriends were," he added.

"You heard the man," Riley said to Julianne. "Let's go."

Julianne rose, but her attention was focused on the lone photograph on the second bulletin board. "I thought that—"

He didn't let her finish. "You thought wrong. We're going to do this in order."

"The first forty-eight hours after a crime are the most crucial."

He didn't want her investigating her cousin's death for a number of reasons, not the least of which was that she was too involved and could very possibly make an emotional call. "Thank you, I'll try to remember that. Now get going. Sanchez, Hill, you take the next two."

"How come we get two and they get one?" Hill protested.

"What is this, kindergarten?" Frank challenged. "The next two are prostitutes. There are less people to talk to."

Hill grunted as he went out with Sanchez, clutching his wilted coffee container.

Frank was right.

The prostitutes proved to be harder to get a handle on. Although some of the working girls staked out particular corners and guarded them zealously, for the most part, the faces along the "Boulevard of Easy Virtue," the label that McFadden had come to be known by, changed. Hookers moved around, they dropped out of sight and no one seemed to notice their absence. If they did, they weren't talking.

Despite having two sets of steps to retrace, Sanchez and Hill were back in the office before Julianne and Riley.

Julianne had expected Frank to allow her to question the various strolling hostesses of the evening about Mary and was disappointed when he'd told her to check out Andrea Katz. The killer's first victim had been a software programmer supposedly away on a business trip when she was killed. She never made it to the meeting that her firm had sent her to.

Andrea, blond, shapely and in her late twenties, had been missing for almost a week before the connection was made between her and the body found in a Dumpster within a trendy apartment complex.

Up until that point, the detectives handling the case assumed that the woman lived within the complex. The fact that no one recognized her only testified to the transient nature of the residents who lived there. People came and went without taking note of one another.

Andrea had been strangled from behind. Like all the victims who came after her.

The people at Andrea's firm had nothing new to add to the testimony they had given before. Andrea was a hard worker, a go-getter who kept to herself for the most part. The people who worked closest to her desk said that there'd been no photographs on it, no treasured mementos. She was very orderly, very neat, almost pathologically so, according to one woman. She made it evident that there was no love lost between them.

"Andrea didn't go out for drinks after work, didn't share lunch with anyone—Lord knows we asked and tried to get her to come, but she always said no. So we stopped asking. She was too interested in getting ahead to make friends," the woman concluded dismissively.

Her testimony echoed that of the other coworkers.

"Makes you think of Thoreau, doesn't it," Riley commented as they left the building and walked up to the car she'd driven to the firm. Julianne looked at her silently, waiting for enlightenment. "You know, the guy who said that most people live lives of quiet desperation."

Julianne shrugged. Other than being an overachiever, there was nothing to set the woman's life apart, nothing that made her a prime target.

"Maybe she liked a quiet life," Julianne speculated. "It wasn't as if someone was holding a gun to her head, saying she had to be a top-notch programmer. It was what she wanted. This day and age, women have a lot more options opened to them than they used to."

Getting into the vehicle, Riley strapped in, waiting

for Julianne to do the same before she started the car. "And yet," she commented, "some of them still choose to go the easy route and sell their bodies for money."

Julianne felt her throat tightening. "What makes you think it's easy?" she challenged.

Riley spared her a glance. "I meant that they didn't have to spend time studying, or sacrificing anything."

Riley couldn't have been more wrong, Julianne thought. She'd come away from questioning the hookers last night with a very distinct impression. It killed her that Mary had numbered among those lost souls. "They sacrificed their pride, their self-respect. They sacrificed everything just to survive. And sometimes, they *do* have guns held to their heads."

"Did I just offend you somehow?" Riley asked. "If I did, I didn't mean it. I was just talking. Thinking out loud."

Julianne blew out a breath. She had no right biting Riley's head off. Riley was right, she hadn't meant anything by it. "Sorry, I'm just edgy."

Riley made a right turn at the next light. "Yeah, I kind of noticed."

It wasn't often she apologized. Wasn't often she felt she was in the wrong. But she had and she was. She supposed some kind of an explanation was in order. "I'm not used to having a partner. The police department over at Mission Ridge isn't very big. I usually go off on my own."

She'd had her suspicions about that, Riley thought. "That kind of thing is frowned upon around here," Riley warned her. And then she winked. "Although it does happen. I'll try not to get on your nerves," she went on to promise amiably.

Julianne looked straight ahead. "It's not you, it's me."

Stopping at a red light, Riley turned toward her, humor curving her mouth at hearing the classic line. "Are you breaking up with me, Julianne?"

Julianne laughed. God, it felt good to laugh. She couldn't remember when she last had. "No, just trying not to be so on edge." Even her hands were clenched in her lap, she realized. She deliberately spread her fingers out in a effort to shed the tension she felt.

Riley inclined her head. "Homicide'll do that to you."

Riley sounded completely laidback and relaxed, Julianne noted. "Doesn't do that to you."

Grinning, Riley lifted one shoulder in a careless little shrug. "I'm one of the lucky ones. I've got a great support system."

"Your family." It wasn't a guess on Julianne's part, not after watching Riley at Rafferty's last night.

Riley nodded. "Nothing beats it."

A sliver of envy momentarily wove its way through her. Had to be nice, Julianne thought, knowing people cared about you. Her father had, in his own way, when he wasn't floating in the bottom of a bottle. "I wouldn't know."

"No family?" Riley asked, surprised.

Julianne thought of Mary, thought of the way her cousin had looked in the Dumpster, her face forever frozen in fear. Had Mary called out to her? With her last breath, had she called to her to come save her the way she used to do when they were both growing up on the reservation? Mary always managed to get into some kind of scrape and then she'd come running for help.

She hadn't been there for Mary when it counted. There was no getting around that.

"No," Julianne finally said flatly.

Riley looked at her, puzzled. "But you're a Navajo, right?"

"Yes."

Riley searched for the right words, not wanting to give any offense. Afraid of treading on feelings that already seemed rather raw. "But isn't the tribe supposed to—"

"Be my family?" Julianne guessed where her partner was going with this. "Ideally. But it doesn't always turn out that way."

Riley was quiet for a long moment, taking advantage of another red light to look at the woman seated next to her. The light changed and she shifted her foot back to the gas pedal.

"Uncle Andrew's going to want to see you," she finally said to Julianne.

"Uncle Andrew?" Julianne echoed. She'd heard several of the Cavanaughs referring to the man last night with more than a little respect. "Is that anything like Marlon Brando in *The Godfather?*"

Riley laughed. "Not hardly. And for the record, he's not really my uncle, although it feels nice to call him that. I did sort of inherited him when my mother married Brian." She slowed down to merge into the next lane, allowing an SUV to pass first. "I'm talking about Andrew Cavanaugh. He used to be the chief of police in Aurora until he retired early to raise his kids." Glancing at Julianne, she noticed that she had the detective's full attention. "His wife disappeared, leaving him with five kids."

Julianne immediately thought of her mother. "She walked out on the family?"

"No, she left for the store and just didn't come back. Actually they thought she was dead. They found her car in the lake. Everything pointed to her accidentally driving off the road."

"But it was murder?" Julianne guessed, picking up on Riley's phrasing.

"No, turns out she actually survived the accident. Rose dragged herself out of the lake, but she'd hit her head and couldn't remember who she was." Even talking about it brought a chill down her back. She didn't know what she'd do if that had been her mother. "A Good Samaritan traveling north took her to a hospital. For the next eleven years, she was someone else, a waitress who worked in a diner up north. Andrew was the only one who didn't think she was dead. He used every spare minute he had to go over and over the evidence."

"Did he ever find her?" Stupid question, Julianne admonished herself. Of course he had, otherwise how would Riley have known the woman had amnesia or where she was all that time.

Riley grinned. "You can meet her at breakfast tomorrow."

Riley was taking an awful lot for granted here. "I can't just barge in—"

Riley stopped her before she could get any further with her protest. "That's just it, you wouldn't be. Uncle Andrew likes to have family over for breakfasts. His family refers to it as 'command performances.' He has this industrial-type stove and is able to make breakfast for veritable legions of people. There're always people at his table and he likes it that way," she concluded as if that was the end of the discussion.

"I'm not family," Julianne pointed out.

"You're a cop, that's family enough for him." She slanted another glance in her direction. "It might make you feel better."

"Thanks, I'll think about it." She had no intention of either thinking about it, or showing up, but it seemed like a polite way to end the conversation.

She'd underestimated her partner.

"I can swing by in the morning, pick you up," Riley volunteered, convinced that the woman would do well to interact with Andrew. "Or Frank can…"

"I'll give you a call if I decide to go," Julianne told her, keeping her tone friendly but firm. She had no desire to mingle with anyone. She wanted to mourn her cousin's passing, find her killer and go back to where she came from. Where people knew not to intrude into other people's lives unless invited.

Frank pushed himself away from his desk. Squaring his shoulders, he pulled them back, stretching muscles that had gotten cramped as he'd hunched over his keyboard. No doubt he would find the serial killer way before he learned how to type quickly.

There was definitely too much paperwork that went with this position. It had been bad enough when he was one of the regular detectives. Now he was drowning in it.

This leader of the pack had more cons than pros, he thought.

He was the last one left again, he noted, looking out at the squad room through the glass partition. And then he stopped.

Someone else was in the squad room.

The lights had dimmed and he'd almost missed her. White Bear. Typing something on the keyboard.

He put his computer to bed and got up. Leaving the tiny cubicle that served as his office, he crossed over to her desk. She was so intent on what she was doing, she didn't seem to hear him.

"So you do know how to use the computer."

Julianne's head jerked up. Frank stood over her desk. Again. Didn't the man have anything better to do? She'd heard that he was quite the ladies' man. Didn't he have any ladies to impress?

"Didn't say I didn't know how to use it," she answered, lowering her eyes back to the keyboard. "I just don't like using it."

So why was she still here? "The shift's over," he told her. "You can go home."

Julianne didn't bother looking up. She went on typing. Faster than he could, he noted. "It's a hotel room."

So, it was like that, was it? He could play along. "Okay, you can go to your hotel room. Or better yet, Rafferty's if you don't want to think. There's enough noise there to freeze your brain."

Julianne raised her eyes to his and he caught himself thinking how beautiful she was.

Her voice was low and devoid of emotion. "What makes you think I don't want to think?"

It amazed him that the woman wasn't stoop-shouldered from the weight of the chip she carried around with her. They both knew the answer to that question. If he had lost a cousin—his only family—he wouldn't want any free time to think, either. Not until he could handle the grief.

Frank debated saying as much, then decided that it wouldn't do any good. The only thing that possibly would could be summarized in two words.

"I'm sorry."

Julianne shrugged, trying to seem nonchalant. "You didn't say anything that—"

"I'm sorry about your cousin."

Julianne lapsed into silence as myriad sensations and emotions warred within her. Her first inclination was just to snap at him, to tell him that she didn't need his pity or whatever it was he was offering, and neither did Mary.

But that would have been wrong. McIntyre was just trying to be nice. Julianne sighed. She supposed she should give him points for that. She was just too thin-skinned lately and would have to adjust.

"Yeah, me, too," she answered quietly. Pressing her lips together, she tried to keep the words back. But maybe, just this once, it wouldn't hurt to share things. For Mary's sake. She didn't want him thinking of her as just some ignorant little runaway who turned tricks to get by. "I wish you could have seen her when she was little. She was always so happy. Always tagging after me." A sad smile played on her lips. She could feel the tears gathering in her eyes. Talking was a mistake. "She thought of me as her big sister, I guess."

It didn't take a rocket scientist to see she was beating

herself up about her cousin's death. "You're not responsible for what happened to her."

"Yes I am," she shouted back, her temper cracking. "All I thought about was me. About making some kind of life for myself. About not winding up like my father. I didn't think about her and what she was going through, didn't even consider the possibility that she might have been living in some kind of hell." Julianne stopped then, covering her mouth with her hands before more words came spilling out. "I'm sorry," she said hoarsely. "I didn't mean to yell."

He waved his hand at the apology, as if the fact that it was unnecessary was a given.

"Beating yourself up isn't going to change anything," he told her. "It's not going to bring her back." He looked at her meaningfully. "And it's not going to help you catch the killer."

She looked away. Seeing Mary in her mind's eye. "No," she agreed in a hoarse whisper, "it's not."

"Shut down your computer, White Bear," he ordered abruptly, making a decision. After all, he was responsible for the welfare of his task force, and this newest member was in serious need of an intervention. "I'm taking you out for a drink."

"I don't drink," she told him flatly. There was no need for the man to do anything. She was responsible for herself.

Rather than come up with alternatives the way his sister had done, Frank looked at the woman before him incredulously. Everyone he knew drank. Not to the point where they were a danger to themselves and others, but everyone liked to unwind by imbibing something with a kick, however minor.

"But I saw you at Rafferty's last night," he protested.

"And I was drinking a ginger ale," Julianne informed him.

He'd seen the color of her drink and had assumed it was a beer, his sister's beverage of choice at Rafferty's. Apparently he was wrong. "Okay, your secret's safe with me. You can have another ginger ale."

Julianne remained where she was. "What is it about your family that makes you all want to pull people out of their nice, dark corners and drag them into loud, noisy places?"

"We're all terminally social," he said matter-of-factly without missing a beat. Deliberately reaching over her desk, he closed the folder that lay open. "Serial killers, though, tend to be loners."

So now he was equating her to a serial killer in waiting? "Not all loners are serial killers."

"No," he agreed amiably, "but all loners run a greater risk of becoming serial killers. They lack the skills for successful interaction with people."

She glanced at the bulletin board as she finally rose from her desk. "I don't know about that. I think our killer has skills. Skills that help him get his victims to lower their guard. Either that, or they all knew the killer."

He turned around and scrutinized the bulletin board, trying to see what made her think so. "What makes you say that?"

She recalled the medical examiner's reports she'd read. "None of the victims had any skin under their nails. There were no defensive wounds. No one fought for their life. The most we have is a frozen look of surprise on a couple of the victims' faces."

He put his hand on her back, gently guiding her out the door. She felt small and delicate under his hand. And she'd probably carve his heart out with some kind of an ancient Navajo ceremonial knife if he said that out loud.

"You're going to have to come up with something more than that to wiggle out of going to Rafferty's," he told her.

"What if I tell you I just don't want to go?" she challenged.

"Overruled, White Bear," he said glibly. "I'm team leader and I say you need to." He eyed her sternly. "Remember, I have the power to have you removed."

She blew out a breath as she crossed the threshold. "Blackmail. Nice."

Frank grinned as he shut off the lights and closed the door. "I thought so."

Chapter 6

"You weren't at your hotel room when I swung by this morning."

Completely lost in the files on her desk, it was all Julianne could do to keep from jumping at the unexpected sound of Frank's voice.

He was just walking into the room.

Julianne stifled a sigh. Miscalculated again. She'd hoped to buy herself a little time alone before anyone showed up in the office. It was a lot easier for her to think when there were no distractions. And although she hated to admit it, McIntyre was proving to be a major distraction. Sanchez and Hill usually strolled in on time, if not late. And this morning, because he'd talked about it yesterday, she'd assumed that both McIntyre and his sister would be busy attending a command breakfast with Andrew Cavanaugh and their wildly extended family.

So much for the best laid plans of mice, men and one struggling police detective trying to catch a break. Or find one, she added silently.

"No, I wasn't. I was here," she answered, pointing out the obvious. Then, because her comment sounded a little sarcastic, even to her own ear, she added, "I thought I'd get an early start." And then, just like that, his words replayed themselves in her head. "Wait, you know where I'm staying?" She didn't remember telling him the name of the hotel. She eyed Frank suspiciously, hating her privacy invaded. The city was littered with hotels and motels. Knowing which one was hers hadn't been just a case of pure luck. "How?"

"I'm team leader. I know everything," he cracked.

She raised her chin. Okay, she'd let the fact that he snooped into her life pass. This was only a minor infraction.

"If you know *everything,* then you have to know that I prefer taking my breakfast alone."

He gave her a tolerant smile. "Just because I know doesn't mean I agree."

Which meant that he still thought it was a good idea to socialize her and he fully intended to. In their off hours. For now, he nodded at the folders spread out all over her desk. It didn't take a genius to guess that she was searching for the common thread. They all were.

"Find anything?" he asked.

"Not yet," she admitted grudgingly. "Re-creating these women's last day doesn't point us in any common direction." Her expression was grim. She hated being stumped. Granted, she'd never been involved in anything of this magnitude before, but that didn't change the ground rules. She *needed* to resolve this. "They didn't all pass by the same place, didn't do anything alike from what I can see. Not to mention that the career professionals had absolutely nothing in common with the street vendors."

Frank's dark brows drew together. "Street vendors?" he echoed, puzzled.

"I'm having a little difficulty calling them what they were, considering that Mary was one of them. I can't picture her letting anyone touch her, not after…" Her voice trailed off and she looked away. Her shoulders lifted and lowered in a defensive, careless shrug.

It didn't take much for Frank to understand what she was going through. If a member of his family had been reduced to Mary's tragic circumstances, he would have handled the situation with a great deal less calm than White Bear appeared to be doing.

"Say the word and you can be off this case."

She began to understand him a little. It was an offer tendered in kindness, not because of some rules and regulations written down in a book. She knew that, heard that, and yet, she couldn't control the way her answer came out.

"No!" Julianne snapped.

He really hadn't expected her to say anything else, he just wanted her to know there was no shame in bowing out.

"Then if you want to do Mary and all these other

dead women any good—" he waved a hand in the general direction of the bulletin boards "—you're going to have to handle it and her murder like anything else you've come across."

He saw Julianne square her shoulders. The thought that she looked like a warrior princess about to go out into the field crossed his mind. So did the word *magnificent*.

"Won't happen again," she promised stoically.

"What? You being human?" Because that was what her reaction was like, pure and simple. "I'm not asking you to be a robot, White Bear, just to keep your personal feelings out of it." Without intending to, he moved in a little closer. So close that there was less than space enough for a deep breath between them. "Save them for something else," he told her, his eyes holding hers. Frank lowered his voice. "Something important."

Damn, but the woman was just *too* attractive. It hit him sometimes, as if it was a new perception on his part instead of something he'd already noted more than once and, basically, right from the start. If he'd run into her anywhere else but on his own task force, there was more than a strong possibility that by now, he would have worn down her barriers and gotten to know the real Julianne White Bear. The one hidden behind all that barbed wire and harsh rhetoric.

It was something that he was looking forward to. Later.

Julianne let out a long, slow breath. Working in this office would be a great deal smoother if McIntyre was old and balding. Or at the very least, married with six kids and battling a bad case of terminal halitosis.

Didn't matter what he looked like, or that, at this

distance, the very breath he exhaled drew her in. She was entirely focused on finding Mary's killer….

And yet, if she were being honest with herself—and she had to be—there was something that was going on here, a strong undercurrent of—what?—she wasn't sure.

With steely resolve, she replied, "I'll keep that in mind."

"Keep what in mind?" Riley asked, walking into the squad room.

Surprised, Frank turned to her. "I thought you'd be here later." She couldn't have already eaten. Even toast at Andrew's table took time. Conversations engulfed people like quicksand. No one got out in under half an hour. "Didn't you stop by Andrew's?"

"Got up late," Riley explained. "If I went by Andrew's, there's no telling how late I would be." She draped her jacket over the back of her chair and dropped her purse into her drawer. "Besides, there are always so many people there, I don't think he'd notice if I didn't show up."

Frank gave her a dubious look. "From what I hear, Andrew notices everything, including who *isn't* there. Story has it that the man's got one of these minds that records everything and plays it back at will."

Unfazed, Riley countered, "He was also a cop. He understands being consumed by a case that just won't open up." She looked from her brother to Julianne. "Did I interrupt something?"

"Saved me from something, actually," Julianne answered quickly. "The 'team leader' was in the middle of giving me a lecture."

"He's good at that," Riley commented. "Years of

being the youngest and having to take everything the rest of us dished out undoubtedly had him storing up a lot of lectures." She smiled at her brother, giving his face an affectionate pat before he pulled back. "Don't get carried away. We need every single body we can get. Live bodies," she qualified, looking at Julianne. They'd started going over the women's apartments yesterday but were by no means finished. "Want to hit the streets, or sit here and listen to Frank pontificate?"

She hardly finished her question before Julianne was reaching for her jacket. "Did you really have to ask?"

Riley laughed. "No, I guess not. Streets it is," she declared, pulling out her car keys. "I'll drive."

Since she didn't know her way around yet, that only made sense, Julianne thought. "No problem."

Her answer drifted back to him as she and his sister left the room.

No problem.

But there was a big problem, Frank, thought as he watched as Julianne make her way down the hall next to Riley. The detective loaned out from Mission Ridge was getting to him. Through no fault of her own, or his.

Tamping down any further thoughts, he went to get a cup of coffee. His stomach rumbled, making him acutely aware that there were consequences to skipping out on one of Andrew's breakfasts.

The smell of despair was everywhere within the four-story pre-1950s walk-up. In the dark hallways with its peeling paint and its scribbled obscenities, echoing in the cries of neglected babies and rising up in the acrid odor of human waste. She was accustomed to poverty. She wasn't accustomed to this.

"Even a dog knows not to go where he sleeps," she murmured under her breath.

"Dogs are smarter than some people," Riley answered.

Julianne did her best not to shiver as she followed Riley into the run-down one-room apartment. The place had once belonged to Rachel Reed, the first prostitute to have made the serial killer's list.

The building was located in the poorer section of Aurora. Here the sun never shone, she thought. Here were housed the hopeless and the just barely not homeless, trying to hang on for just another day until they either died or somehow wandered into the path of a stray miracle. Either way, their misery would be over.

Had Mary lived in such a place? Or was this horrid place actually something she would have aspired to? Mary might have huddled somewhere out on the street, fighting for a space that had no vermin, no bugs that would crawl along her body while she slept.

Oh God, Mary, why didn't I take you with me? I'm sorry, so sorry.

Riley glanced in her direction, interpreting her reaction. "Pretty grim, isn't it? Hard to picture someone actually living like this."

"Yeah," was all Julianne permitted herself to say. And then she looked at Riley. "How can you sound so upbeat?" she asked. The woman sounded as if none of this, the squalor, the wasted lives affected her on any significant level.

"Because if I let it get to me," Riley answered simply,

"I don't function. And these women need me to function so that I can get the bastard who cut them down in the prime of their lives." That said, she started to go through the prostitute's meager belongings. "Well, let's see if there's something that might have been missed the first time," Riley murmured. Sanchez and Hill had gone over the one-room apartment initially. There was always hope something had been overlooked. "Not much to see," she speculated. "Shouldn't take us too long."

"Hard to believe that this is the sum total of someone's life," Julianne murmured, opening up the single, narrow closet. Only a few items of clothing were hanging inside.

Riley and Julianne methodically went through everything, including the miniature refrigerator. They were finished almost before they started. There wasn't much in the apartment. No books, no signs that this was anything but a place for the victim to put her head down, except for the television set.

Julianne paused in front of it the old-fashioned analog type TV with rabbit ears. Possibly left behind by a previous tenant, she judged. She turned it on. Nothing but snow appeared on the screen even when she flipped to a few different channels. It seemed to emphasize that there was nothing in the victim's life. She shut the set again.

A couple of fliers the woman might have picked up along the way were on top of the set. One from a homeless shelter somewhere in the vicinity, the other from a fast-food place she noted was around the corner.

"Nothing," Riley sighed, shaking her head as she finished going through a rickety bureau that contained several pairs of undergarments, some sweaters and a graduation yearbook that was several years old. The victim's, or was it something she'd stolen? She decided it might bear a look. Turning, she glanced over at the dark-haired woman across the room. "Anything stand out for you?"

Julianne looked around at the dust and dirt. "Only that she wasn't a very good housekeeper."

Riley grinned. "Well, if that was a crime, the jails would be *really* overcrowded." Picking up the yearbook, she gave the place one last scan. "Might as well get back."

"Drop me off at McFadden," Julianne told her as Riley closed up the apartment. The boulevard was only a few blocks away from where they were right now.

"Why?" Riley asked as they started back down the stairs. "What's there?"

Maybe she'd gotten her information wrong. "Isn't that the place where most of the prostitutes gather?"

"Not so much before dusk."

"Still, there might be some out, getting an early start and who knows, someone might have seen something suspicious."

"We've already canvassed the area," Riley pointed out. "Right after each hooker was found."

"Can't hurt to show some of the photographs around again." She was thinking of the copy she had with her of Mary's photo. "Maybe you missed talking to one of them, someone who could remember a detail." She was grasping at straws, but stranger things had happened. "And it's not like we have any leads to chase down," Julianne told her.

Riley thought it over. "Okay, we'll both go. It'll go faster that way," she theorized. About to get into her car, she heard her cell phone going off. Half a beat later, so did Julianne's.

"McIntyre."

"White Bear."

Riley looked over the roof of her vehicle at Julianne. It was obvious that they were getting the same call from two difference sources. She saw the other woman's eyes widen. And then she heard why.

"Two?" Riley echoed in disbelief. She struggled to keep the horror out of her voice.

But Julianne heard her and she nodded as she closed her cell phone and slipped it into the pocket of her jacket. "That's what the man said. I think our killer is looking for a greater high," Julianne said grimly. The deaths were happening closer together. According to the files, the first had been almost a year ago. Now only days separated one from another.

The killer's bloodlust was growing.

Riley started the car. McFadden was going to have to wait. They had a date with two Dumpsters. "Either that, or he's enjoying rubbing our noses in it."

Julianne shook her head. Something in her gut told her that it wasn't that. "It's not about us, I don't think. It's about them. His victims."

Riley looked at her sharply. "You found something you want to share?"

Something had occurred to her, but she wasn't ready to elaborate just yet. "I'll let you know after we see the latest victims." Even as she said it, she started to brace herself for the ordeal that lay ahead. She glanced at Riley's profile and saw her own feelings reflected in the set of the woman's jaw. She remembered what Riley'd said to her. "It doesn't get easier, does it?"

"Nope," Riley replied as she turned on the siren. "It really doesn't."

Victims number eight and nine were both very successful in their chosen fields. Zoe Martin was a criminal lawyer from one of the more renowned law firms in the country and Christina Wayne was an interior decorator with her own business and a client list that extended to the rich and famous—the very rich and famous.

Their bodies were discovered buried beneath a thin layer of debris in two different Dumpsters arranged side by side behind one of the fancier hotels located in the heart of the city. The debris was not meant to hide them so much as to highlight the fact that, like the rotting food and refuse, the dead women were trash, too.

The crime-scene investigators, three of them, were already on the scene when she and Riley arrived. As was Frank. Sanchez and Hill were just pulling up.

Julianne got out and strode over to the first Dumpster. Steeling herself off, she climbed up and looked in, virtually over the shoulder of one of the crime-scene investigators. Without a word, she climbed down and then went to the second Dumpster. The second C.S.I. had just finished taking pictures.

The second woman had been tossed in just like the first, as if she was nothing more than just trash, not even worthy of an afterthought. God, but this was one cold S.O.B. they were dealing with, she thought grimly.

"Well?" Riley asked as Julianne moved away from the second Dumpster.

"Well what?" Frank asked. He'd crossed over to them and caught the expectant note in his sister's voice.

Riley turned toward him, more than willing to share. "Julianne thinks she might have a theory about our serial killer."

"Okay, let's hear it," Frank said. "At this point, I'm ready to go with anything if it makes the slightest bit of sense."

"He's killing the same woman," Julianne told him, trying in vain to distance herself from what she'd just seen. Like Mary, these women were going to haunt her for a very long time.

Frank looked at her. "What do you mean, the same woman?"

What had set her thinking along this path was Mary's wig. "They all have the same coloring, are approximately the same age—give or take. Somewhere along the line, our killer was rejected by a blond-haired, blue-eyed woman with high cheekbones and undoubtedly higher standards. Standards that he didn't measure up to. Mary had black hair, but you found a blond wig in the Dumpster with her. Maybe she was trying to disguise herself, to pretend to herself that it wasn't her. The point is, this guy's got it in for blondes. Rejection seems to be the likely conclusion."

"So if he's taking revenge, why didn't he rape them?" Riley asked.

It was a good question, and she only had a partial answer. "Maybe he thought that was withholding the ultimate intimacy, something he's not capable of or didn't want to share."

There was merit in the thought, Frank decided. "You think it all started with the first victim? That she was his real target and he just got carried away?" he asked her.

She hadn't worked that out yet. "Maybe. Maybe not. Maybe he didn't have enough courage to kill the woman who actually rejected him. Could have been a girlfriend, could have been his mother, but somewhere along the line, she rejected him and he's been nursing his wounds until now." She moved out of the way as another C.S.I. set down a plastic marker to denote where a piece of jewelry was found on the ground. "Once started, he kept taking his frustrations out on the surrogates he's been picking out."

"Why now?" Frank posed. "Why not earlier? What makes now different?"

Again, she had no answers except this feeling in her gut. She shook her head. "Some kind of trigger. A meltdown, a personal tragedy, I don't know, but something set him off and he's not going to stop until we stop him. Which means there'll probably be more dead women."

Even as she said the words, Julianne had to struggle not to shiver.

Chapter 7

Frank looked at the woman before him thoughtfully. Obviously, there was more to her than just an undercurrent of sensuality and quiet beauty.

"That's pretty good," he finally acknowledged. "Ever consider working as a profiler?"

"For the FBI?" Even as she asked, Julianne shook her head. The bureau was the last place she'd want to work. "Too many rules and regulations."

That was an odd thing to say, Frank thought, considering her present position. "And being a police detective has less?"

It all depended on whether you worked in the big city, or a small township. She'd chosen accordingly. "In Mission Ridge it does. Captain Randolph gives me pretty much free rein. But then, there's hardly any crime in Mission Ridge." Which could account for the lax regulations. It wasn't a matter of "them" versus "us." To a greater extent, they were all just neighbors with jobs to do. "Kids joyriding once in a while. Lawn sculptures placed in suggestive poses, things like that."

He'd thought places like that only existed in idyllic novels. "I can see why you wouldn't have wanted to have a dead body on your hands. Spoils paradise."

Paradise. She'd never thought of Mission Ridge in those terms. "Wouldn't exactly call it that," she told him. "In my experience, paradise doesn't exist. There're too many people around out for only themselves for that to happen." Even in Mission Ridge. After all, her uncle had lived on the outskirts of the town.

One rotten apple …

Definitely in need of Cavanaugh exposure, Frank judged, looking at Julianne. And as soon as possible. The woman with the incredible blue eyes was in pain, whether she realized it or not. And he hated seeing anyone in pain. The fact that he was attracted to her would have to be put on hold. Helping her, however, was necessary, what he needed to do.

He still had a crazed serial killer on his hands, not to mention a new, double homicide to contend with. He had a gut feeling that the new victims weren't taken and killed at the same time. One victim had to precede the other, the medical examiner would sort out.

And it was up to them to do everything else.

"Okay, people, you know the drill," Frank announced, raising his voice so that Hill and Sanchez could hear him as well. "Canvas the area. Talk to everyone with a pulse. Somebody *has* to have seen something," he insisted. "This bastard can't continue being the luckiest S.O.B. on the face of the earth. His luck has to run out some time." When he saw Riley begin to leave with Julianne, he called out, "Wait up." Both women turned around, waiting for him to give them further instructions. "White Bear, you're with me. Riley, get the names of the hotel guests on the second and third floors facing the alley. I want them all giving statements."

With that, Frank quickly walked out of the alley. Julianne hurried after him. The man had freakishly long legs, she thought, having almost to run in order to catch up.

"Don't trust me?" she asked when she was finally abreast of him. Was that why he suddenly had her pairing up with him?

He gave her a look that told her she was off base. "I like to rotate positions when I work," was all he said to her.

She knew there had to be more and, because she was the outsider, she was pretty certain that her first assessment was accurate. He wanted to keep an eye on her. Something she'd done or said had gotten under his skin.

For the moment, she played along with his answer. "Too bad, your sister and I were beginning to hit a routine."

"Now you can hit a routine with me." He stood back and let her go through the hotel's revolving door first. Except that she didn't. Stepping to the side, she pulled open the door that was on the side.

Everything she did made him wonder about her. This was no exception. But for now, a desk clerk needed questioning and an initial report compiling. His own, personal questions were just going to have to wait.

When the task force finally made it back to the squad room several hours later, Brian Cavanaugh was waiting for them. With him was a solemn-faced, dark-haired man who looked as if he'd emerged from a standard government agency cookie press. He had on a black suit, a white shirt and appeared to Julianne as if his face had never entertained even a glimmer of a smile in his forty-something years on the planet.

Brian made the introductions quickly. "This is Special Agent Elliot Solis," he said, then pointed out each of his detectives by name, refraining from mentioning that his stepson and daughter were in the group. Julianne was introduced separately, with an addendum that she was on loan from a neighboring town. "I was just showing him the task force area."

Frank was instantly on guard. There was only one reason the FBI would send one of their agents. "Are you here to take over?"

Julianne glanced at him. He was being territorial. She could understand that. It gave them something in common.

The man's expression remained unchanged. "No, just to give you the benefit of my expertise."

"You're a profiler," Julianne guessed, her voice just as expressionless as his face.

"Yes, I am. And Chief Cavanaugh has been filling me in on the case." Julianne thought she detected a touch of elitism in his tone. She wondered if Frank took offense at it. He must.

The special agent looked at the bulletin boards. Sanchez was just tacking up the two latest photographs beside the lone photograph that bore silent testimony to Mary's murder. Until they located better photographs, the ones taken at the dump site of the last two would have to do.

"He's escalating," Solis commented.

Frank folded his arms before him. He reminded her of a portrait of a warrior she'd once seen. "Certainly looks that way," he agreed stoically.

Moving toward the bulletin boards, Solis glanced from one photograph to another in silence, then turned around. He wasted no time in rendering his profile.

"Most likely, you're searching for a loner, someone who's always been on the outside, looking in. He's white, between the ages of late twenties to early forties and he has trouble holding down a job. He might even be homeless, which just feeds his rage." As he spoke, he looked from one detective to another, as if to watch his words sink in. "Women won't give him the time of day and he's sexually frustrated." The FBI profiler stopped. "You're frowning, detective." His observation was addressed to Julianne. "Something I said?"

She didn't like being singled out, especially since she really wasn't part of the group. It made her feel as if she was on a tightrope. But Solis was expecting an answer, so she gave him one—in the form of a question. "Are you aware that none of the women were raped, Special Agent?"

Unfazed, Solis shrugged his shoulders. His black jacket barely moved. "Just means he's impotent, that's all. More to be angry about."

She didn't think so. "No, if he were impotent and this was about sexual rage, he'd used anything he could get his hands on to penetrate them. Rebar, a stick, a bottle, whatever did the trick if that was his ultimate goal. Plenty of things like that in the Dumpsters—and most likely wherever the murder happened." Because, like Frank, she subscribed to the theory that all the women were killed somewhere other than where they were found.

It was obvious that Solis wasn't pleased with her take on it. "So what are you saying, he's 'respectfully' murdering them?"

She wished she hadn't started this. But if the special agent intended on making her squirm, he was going to be disappointed, she thought. "No, I'm saying that maybe he's just trying to get rid of them, to rid the world of them," she elaborated, and then added, "And I don't think he's homeless."

The man's eyebrows rose as he pinned her with a skeptical look. It was all Frank could do to keep from laughing.

"Oh?"

Julianne forged ahead, even though she fought back an urge to tell the profiler what he could so with his high-handed, disapproving tone.

"More than half the women are professional career women. They'd never let a homeless man near them. Neither would the prostitutes." She saw Riley look at her in surprise. "Homeless men don't have the kind of money the hookers are looking to make."

Solis snorted, dismissing her theory. "And how long have you been profiling?"

"About an hour," she answered evenly. "But I've been

observing people for a lot longer than that," she added just as a smug expression began to come over the man's angular face.

Sensing that they were on the verge of having the situation become *really* uncomfortable, Brian quickly intervened.

"Special Agent Solis, are you going to be sticking around to help us with this case?" Forewarned was forearmed, he'd always believed. The man had said nothing about this possibility when he'd arrived, so Brian was hoping the answer to his question was no.

And it was. "Sorry, but I've got to be getting back," Solis told him. "I was just asked to come out and form a profile of the man you're looking for." He looked pointedly at Julianne. "Now that I have—"

"You need to be getting back to the field office, I completely understand." Without wasting any time and afraid that the man might change his mind, Brian looked over toward Hill. "Detective Hill, would you mind driving Special Agent Solis to the airport?"

Hill looked a little surprised at being chosen, then inclined his head. One outsider was enough to get used to. This one was going to make too many waves in the way they worked.

"No problem." He offered Solis a large, toothy smile. "Come with me, Special Agent."

Once the profiler had left, Brian looked at Julianne. "Well, I was going to ask if you'd found a niche for yourself, but I guess I've got my answer."

Julianne pressed her lips together. At least he wasn't reprimanding her. "I didn't mean to step on any toes, it's just that I don't think that Solis's right. I think whoever this serial killer is, the women trust him. Trust him enough to let them come within five feet of them. That's not someone who's been living on the streets, or gives off vibes that he's sexually frustrated."

Riley picked up on the word Julianne used. "Trust him how? Like a priest?"

Julianne thought about it. "No. Only two of these women were Catholics." The rest were a scattering of different religions and at least one was an avowed atheist. "Why would the others seek out a priest?"

Offhand, there was no answer for that. "So we're back to square one?" Brian asked.

"Not exactly square one," she said. They had learned a few things, she thought. "More like version one point one."

Like software, Brian thought. He supposed it was something. "Keep at it," he said to Frank. "The city's getting very jumpy about having a serial killer in their midst."

Frank knew his stepfather would have rather kept the whole thing under wraps without involving the news media, but the papers broke the story several weeks ago. Since then, they'd set up a tip line. It was almost never silent. And nothing had come of it.

"Maybe that's a good thing," Frank theorized. "It'll make women be more careful."

"Or paranoid," Brian countered. He'd been around long enough to have seen these kinds of things go bad. "That's all I need, a city full of women with concealed weapons, ready to Taser—or worse—the next poor slob who make the mistake of tapping them on the shoulder."

"At least they'll both be alive," Riley pointed out. "And that's a good thing."

"Just get this loony for me," Brian requested with weary feeling. Before leaving, he turned toward Julianne. "And, White Bear?"

She'd been waiting for the chief to get around to her. She had embarrassed a special agent with the FBI and now it was time to pay the piper. Was he going to send her away? "Yes, sir?"

Brian smiled at her warmly. "Nice job just now."

She blinked, confused. Praise was something she was essentially unacquainted with. "Excuse me, sir?"

"Coming up with your own profile," the chief explained, amused by her disoriented expression. "I think yours works better than the one that special agent gave us."

She wasn't sure how to react. Something warm opened up in her chest. "Thank you, sir."

"*Chief* will do," Brian told her. *Sir* made him feel as if he was ready to be put out to pasture. With a new bride at home, out to pasture was definitely one place he wasn't ready to occupy.

"Chief," Julianne echoed with a nod of her head. The corners of her mouth curved ever so slightly.

"Anything else strike you about this man?" Frank asked as soon as his stepfather had left the room.

Julianne shook her head. "Nothing I can think of, offhand." She paused, then added, "Except that maybe he has a nice face."

"A nice face," Frank echoed. "What is that supposed to mean?"

"A nice face," she repeated. "Again, like someone you'd trust. Like someone who looks like he'd never even think of hurting anyone, much less a perfect stranger."

Sanchez joined their circle. "You mean like Ted Bundy?"

The infamous serial killer had been able to conduct his bloodthirsty spree because he was so good-looking and so nonthreatening in appearance. No one suspected him of being capable of the gruesome crimes he actually committed.

Julianne nodded. "Something like that."

"You think this serial killer stalked them?" Frank asked, wondering just how much thought White Bear had put into this and if it all was just speculation on her part, or if she was working with some sort of insider information they didn't know about.

Confronted with the question, Julianne thought for a moment. "I think he comes across them in his daily life and then, yes I think he starts watching them until he feels the time is right."

"And when is the time right?" Riley pressed eagerly, caught up in the theory.

Julianne shook her head, frustrated. "That I don't know."

Frank said nothing as he went back to his office. There was a great deal to think about, though.

He put her on phone duty, explaining that everyone had a turn listening and taking down what eventually turned out to be false pieces of information, usually rendered with the best of intentions.

Several hours of that had all but flattened her ear and made her feel as if she was close to being brain dead. She had a hard time not commenting on obvious stupidity, but somehow, Julianne managed to make it through the shift.

Returning to the squad room for her things, she passed Frank's office. Everyone else had already gone home for the day. Mercifully, there'd been no other sightings, no other bodies discovered in Dumpsters.

In his office, his back was to the entrance and he was on the phone. She was about to knock on his door to give him the courtesy of saying she was leaving.

But since she had no idea how long he was going to be, she turned on her heel, about to leave, when she heard him say, "I appreciate you taking the time to talk to me, Captain Randolph. I'd also appreciate it if you keep this conversation just between the two of us. Right," he said, answering something the man on the other end of the phone said. "I agree. She wouldn't understand. Glad you do, sir. Good night."

All sorts of thoughts ricocheted through her head. The second McIntyre hung up, she charged into his office, ready for a confrontation. Her initial thought had been just to get away. But that never solved anything. Besides, she was mad. Who the hell did he think he was, checking up on her?

"You called Captain Randolph about me?" she demanded hotly.

Startled, Frank swung around in his chair. He

hadn't even heard her walk up. "Julianne, I thought you were gone."

It was the first time she'd heard him say her first name. Somehow, that made everything that had just happened that much more personal. And it made her angrier.

"Well, I'm not!" she snapped. Her hands were on her hips as her eyes flashed blue lightning. "Were you just pumping Captain Randolph for information about me?"

"Just trying to get a few things straight," he answered vaguely, then added, "And I'd tone my voice down a few notches if I were you." He didn't appreciate her tone of voice, no matter how magnificent she looked when angry.

"Well, you're not me," she fired back. "Nobody just delved into your life history—"

He held up a hand to stop her. "Not exactly your life history—"

She charged right over it. "Then *what* 'exactly'?" she demanded, her temper flaring higher. Digging her knuckles into his desk top, she leaned over it, her face inches from his. "What could you have possibly asked the captain that you couldn't ask me firsthand?"

He rose from his desk, his eyes darkening to match his expression. "And if I asked you questions, you would have answered them?"

"Yes!" she snapped at him.

He had his doubts. Everything about the woman was secretive. She played her cards close to the vest. "Truthfully?"

Her eyes widened. The question all but took her breath away. This was her integrity he was bandying about. "So now you suspect I'm a liar as well as whatever else is going on in your mind?"

He backtracked. "I just wanted to be sure about you."

"Sure about what?" she demanded. What was he accusing her of?

"That you were here because he sent you, that you didn't falsify your papers—"

She let him get no further. "Falsify my—" She was too stunned to finish the sentence. "Why the *hell* would I do that?" she cried.

"Because you seemed to know a lot about the killer," he told her honestly. "I thought maybe there was some kind of connection."

"There is." Her voice was dangerously low. "He killed my cousin."

Frank shook his head, dismissing her answer. "I mean more than that."

"Did you also accuse the FBI profiler?" she asked. "He claimed to know what made the serial killer tick. Why didn't you check him out? Why just me?"

"Because you seem to be dead-on." He looked at her for a long moment. Had she seen the killer? When that one woman was murdered in Mission Ridge, had White Bear stumbled across him and let him go for some reason? Had guilt brought her here, and now she wanted to make amends?

"So I'm better at putting some of the pieces together than he is. Is that a crime?" Angry, insulted, Julianne drew herself up. "Look, if you don't want my help, just say the word."

They'd gone around about this thing just the other

day. And she'd asked to stay. Was she changing her mind now? "You'd go back to Mission Ridge?" he asked incredulously.

"No, I'd take some time off and try to find this sicko on my own." And then she allowed sarcasm to enter her voice. "But don't worry, I wouldn't want to interfere with your work."

He didn't respond immediately. Instead, he studied her for a long, unnerving moment.

"Under the heading of 'Works and plays well with others,' did you get straight 'unsatisfactories' when you were in elementary school?" he finally asked her. A hint of a smile played on his lips as he asked.

Julianne tossed her head. "I was a happy kid," she informed him defiantly.

"So what happened?"

He was standing much too close to her. Invading her space. She would have taken a step back if it wouldn't have given him the impression that he intimidated her— because he didn't.

"I grew up."

He watched her mouth as she fired back at him and felt something stir inside. He was more than familiar with the reaction.

Too bad, he lamented silently.

"Takes more than that," he told her. He wanted to know what pressed this woman's buttons. Why she looked as if she was a firecracker about to go off without warning. Maybe if he knew, it would curb his desire to find out what her mouth tasted like. "Tell you what, why don't we grab a drink and we can talk about it?"

What was it with these people and their attention spans? "I told you, I don't—"

"Drink, right, I know. Water, then," he suggested easily. "What we're doing as we talk isn't important. Talking is."

"Frustrated shrink?" she guessed sarcastically at his reasons.

"Frustrated detective." He looked at her pointedly. "Won't cost you to talk to me."

She supposed he wanted to go to his usual place. She didn't. She didn't want to be on display for all the other members of the police department to gap at. "Rafferty's?"

He shrugged. "Or someplace else. The drink and the place don't matter," he emphasized.

Okay, so what would it hurt? If he was determined to spend some time with her after hours, she might as well get something out of it. "All right. You can buy me dinner."

Frank grinned. "Consider it done."

He was grinning. She wished he wouldn't grin. It got to her.

The word *mistake* whispered across her brain as she left the squad room with him.

Chapter 8

Frank brought her to a well-lit family-style restaurant with checkered tablecloths and friendly ambience. The food, although not fancy, was appetizing, and the service was fast.

Ordering a Black Russian for himself, he was surprised when Julianne agreed to the waiter's suggestion of sparkling cider. He watched with interest as Julianne drained her glass while waiting for their dinners to arrive. The waiter came by to refill the glass after setting their meals down in front of them.

For a woman who didn't imbibe, Frank mused, she certainly did do justice to her drink.

He waited until he was fairly certain that Julianne had taken the edge off her hunger before he asked the question that had been on his mind since she first walked into the squad room.

"All right, Detective White Bear, tell me what makes you so angry."

She raised her eyes to his, wondering, at the same time, why the room was just the slightest bit out of focus. "I'm not angry."

He said nothing in response. Instead, he put down his fork and he took out his cell phone. Aiming it at her, he snapped a picture. Then, switching the camera's function to the still mode, he placed his phone on the table and turned it upside down so that she could see it.

"Then I'd say that you're doing a good imitation."

Snapping the phone shut, she pushed it back to him. "Okay," she allowed grudgingly. "Point taken. Maybe, if I look angry," she qualified, not giving in completely, "it's because I don't have any control over where I'm being sent. One day, I'm at Mission Ridge dealing with the city's first homicide in ten years, the next, I'm here, being shoved in with a group of people who all know each other and most likely resent having someone forced on them, but are too polite to say it." She paused, taking another sip to wash down her words before continuing, "Maybe I'm angry because this serial killer found Mary before I could—and took her away forever." She drew in a breath, her head swimming just a little. "And maybe I'm angry because despite the fact that the group leader is invading my space and thinks someone appointed him my social director, I'm so attracted to him, I'm having trouble concentrating."

The moment the words were out of her mouth, she

appeared more surprised than he did to hear them. Eyes widening at what she viewed to be a very basic tactical error, Julianne looked down at the empty glass beside her in awakening horror. "That's not just apple cider, is it?"

Well, that explained that, he thought. Playing along, Frank reached over for her glass and sniffed it.

"Nope," he confirmed. "I'm no expert, but I'd say that was some form of white wine. It does have a hint of apples to it," he allowed, setting the glass back down on the table. He couldn't resist asking, "Couldn't you tell the difference?"

She drew herself up, trying to appear formidable. At five-four and with a slight build, she usually relied on her expression to do the trick. Right now, lightning was all but shooting from her eyes.

It wasn't his fault, she reminded herself, trying to be fair. McIntyre hadn't ordered the drink for her, she had, going with the waiter's suggestion.

"Obviously not." Sighing, she pushed the glass away from her. Locking the barn door after the horses had run away, she thought, upbraiding herself. "I should have told him to bring me a ginger ale." And then, because there was a need to blame someone, she eyed him accusingly. "Did you tell him to switch drinks?"

He didn't take offense. "You were sitting here the entire time. Unless you think I have some kind of secret powers and can communicate with people through telepathy, I think you know the answer to that." And then, because he couldn't help himself, he smiled warmly at her. Regulations dictated that he ignore her confession and pretend that nothing had said about the electricity humming between them. But he was too intrigued, too taken with her to just let her words pass without some sort of acknowledgement. "You're attracted to me?"

She could feel herself reddening and gave him a look that bordered on murderous, deliberately daring him to make a comment about her changing complexion. "It's the wine talking."

His gut told him that this wasn't the case here. "Sometimes alcohol loosens tongues."

Her eyes narrowed. "And sometimes it turns people into useless drunks."

She said it with such feeling, Frank was certain that someone close to her had to be the focus of that statement. A lover? An ex-husband? He'd seen her file and there was next to nothing personal in it. Other than her having grown up on a reservation and the fact that both her parents were deceased, nothing in it gave him a clue about her childhood. He was filling in the blanks as he went.

He leaned forward, lowering his voice. Sounding kind. "Who did it turn into a useless drunk, Julianne?"

There he went again, using her name and making it personal. She wished he'd stop that. She raised her chin defiantly.

"That has no bearing on anything."

"Doesn't it?" he challenged. "We're all made up of a million different little pieces that are fit together. Some of which go back to our childhood," he added tactfully. He saw resistance enter her eyes.

Maybe, if he was lucky, it would be a matter of "I'll

show you mine if you show me yours." It was worth a try. But that meant that he had to go first.

More than most, Frank understood her reluctance about talking about her personal life. He didn't exactly like talking about parts of his past, either. But if his talking about his past would free her up to talk about hers, then it was worth it.

Besides, it wasn't as if no one knew. That was the problem. Too many people knew. It was something he and his brother and sisters, not to mention his mother, had had to live down.

So, when she said nothing, he took the plunge. "I've spent the last few years fighting the specter of my father. Rumor had it that he was a dirty cop, that he was trying to rip off the very people he was supposed to be busting." Talking about it brought back the anger. It surged through him. He wondered if he was ever going to be able to revisit this time without feeling betrayed and defensive. "The worst of it was when they started whispering things about my mother, saying that she was in on his plan, or that she knew where the money that had disappeared was buried. It got me pretty crazy for a while," he admitted.

"How did you handle it?" she asked.

"Instead of getting into fights, defending her, defending his name, I learned how to just ignore what was being said." His expression turned grim as he remembered the events of the previous year. Of how his mother had tried in vain to protect them all from the fall out. "But then my father came back from the dead and everything that had been said about him turned out to be true."

"Wait, wait." Julianne grabbed his hand, as if that would stop him from going any further. Suddenly realizing what she was doing, that her hand was covering his, she pulled it back. "What do you mean, he 'came back from the dead'?"

He was so used to the people around him being aware of the details, he forgot that she wouldn't be. "We all thought he was dead. There'd been a gun battle and my father's mutilated body wound up washing up on the shore. At least, we *thought* it was his body. We held a closed-casket funeral service for him and buried him in the family plot." The ironic smile on his lips had no humor in it. "Turns out it wasn't him. It was his drug contact who was killed in the shoot-out. My father was probably the one who pulled the trigger," he added grimly. "He dressed the other man in his clothes, then bashed his face in. We made a natural mistake."

She knew what it felt like wanting to be proud of your father and knowing that you couldn't be. That he was nothing more than a huge disappointment, a weak man who thought only of himself.

Her sympathy aroused, she looked at him for a long moment. "How did you stand it?"

Frank shrugged. He hadn't intended for his "confession" to go this far. He'd brought her here to find out more about her, not talk about his own past. "You get through it. And it helps to have someone like Brian Cavanaugh on your side," he told her. "Not to mention siblings to turn to."

She thought of the people Riley had introduced her to the other night. She vaguely recalled that a couple of them, a man and a woman, had been named McIntyre. That made him far better off than her.

"Yeah, well, things are different when there's nobody to turn to."

Nobody. That had to be one of the loneliest words he'd ever heard. "Nobody?"

She shook her head. From what she'd heard, her mother, already convinced that she'd made a huge mistake marrying her father, hadn't wanted any children. After she was born, her parents stopped sleeping in the same bed.

"I'm—I was," she amended with a great deal of difficulty, "five years older than Mary. When the bottle finally did my father in, I was a couple of weeks shy of turning eighteen. My uncle volunteered to take me in." Her mouth hardened. "According to him, it was my father's dying wish that I move in with him and my cousin. It didn't sound like my father, but I just wanted to be part of something so much, I believed him. Turned out that it was my uncle's wish, not my father's."

It wasn't hard to pick up on her tone. "What did your uncle do to you?"

"Nothing," she answered firmly, and then she relented, adding, "Not for lack of trying. Every time I walked by, he tried to pull me onto his lap, grab me…" Julianne shrugged, letting the momentary silence take the place of any further explanations. "I lasted exactly eight days, then packed up and left in the middle of the night." If she'd tried in the daytime, she knew her uncle would have tried to physically stop her, and he was twice as big as she was. "I got a job and put myself through school," she continued without any fanfare, then sighed heavily. "It never occurred to me that he would try to do the same thing to his own daughter." Just saying it made her feel ill all over again.

He'd seen it time and again. People who blamed themselves for things they had absolutely no control over. "That's because you don't think like a sick child predator."

"I should have. I should have known," she murmured more to herself than to him. "Now, because of me, Mary's dead." And she was never going to forgive herself for that.

"What happened to your cousin is *not* your fault," Frank insisted firmly. What was it going to take for her to believe him?

"Yes, it is," she answered quietly. There was no way that she couldn't take responsibility for this. "I failed her when she needed me."

Stopping abruptly, Julianne looked at him. Most likely it was the wine talking. But maybe McIntyre was right. Maybe it just loosened tongues instead of fabricated stories.

Julianne leaned in closer and said, "I don't want to be alone tonight."

Her breath was warm on his face and he could feel his pulse accelerating. But even though he felt himself responding to her and to what she was saying in myriad ways, he knew nothing would come of it. Because he wouldn't allow it. He didn't believe in taking advantage of vulnerable women no matter how attracted to them he was. There were rules, rules of his own making, that he followed.

"I'll take you to your hotel room," he told her. "Tomorrow, Riley will come by and bring you to your car," he continued, answering Julianne's question before she could ask.

Signaling for the check, Frank paid the amount in cash, leaving a healthy tip. He slipped his wallet back into his pocket and placed his hand under her arm. "Let's go, Julianne."

"White Bear," she corrected, rising to her feet. "Call me White Bear."

It seemed like an odd request. Usually, a woman who wanted to sleep with you wanted things to be more intimate, not less. "Why?"

Julianne took a breath, trying to keep things from slipping into a haze. "Because when you say my name, it feels too personal." They walked outside and the cool evening air made her feel a little better. "This isn't going to be personal," she informed him.

This was absurd, she thought, annoyed with herself. Why was her head buzzing like this? It was just one stupid glass of wine. Okay, maybe two, she amended, remembering that the waiter had come by to refill her glass. The problem was, she suddenly remembered, that she'd consumed the wine on essentially an empty stomach. And because she blamed it for her parents' breakup, she had never built up any sort of tolerance for alcohol.

A little tolerance would have been wonderful right about now.

They'd reached his vehicle and she realized that he was looking at her. "It's not going to be personal, huh?" It was a rhetorical question.

She began to shake her head, then thought better of it. Her head was throbbing as it was. "Nope."

"Then I take it we're going to be using puppets?" he asked mildly, unlocking her door.

"We're going to be having sex," she retorted, getting into his car. Sinking into the seat, she took a moment undertaking the ordeal of buckling up. "That doesn't have to be personal."

Getting in on the driver's side, Frank laughed shortly. There was a lot that had to be straightened out about this woman.

"Sorry, whenever I make love with a woman, it's *always* personal." He spared her a look before backing out of the parking space. "Otherwise, why bother?"

Confusion wove in and out of her brain as Julianne tried to think. "To release energy, tension," she finally answered.

Wow. He shook his head in disbelief. "You've just reduced a beautiful thing to a science theorem. Bet you have to beat men off with a stick."

She took his last sentence literally. And remembered. "A knife," she corrected.

They were on the road. Rather than pass through the amber light, he slowed down and watched the traffic signal turn red. This wasn't the kind of conversation to be had while staring through the front windshield. "You used a knife?"

She shut her eyes and found that wasn't such a good idea. Things began to swim. She opened her eyes again. "Just once."

To defend herself? To exact revenge? With her, it could have gone either way. He didn't know her well enough to make the actual call, but his gut told him it was probably self-defense. "Want to talk about it?"

The light turned green. He wasn't moving. "No."

The driver behind him tapped his horn. Frank put his foot on the accelerator. His hands tightened ever so slightly on the steering wheel. "He deserve it?"

The laugh gave him his answer before she did. "In spades."

There was silence for the rest of the trip, which wasn't long. Within ten minutes, he was guiding his vehicle into the parking lot. Frank found a spot close to the entrance.

Pulling up the hand brake, he turned the engine off and then looked in her direction. Ordinarily, he would have just waited for her to get out but his gut told him that, despite her pride, Julianne might need a little help navigating. Without saying as much, he got out on his side and rounded the trunk of his car, getting to her door before she had a chance to pull the handle.

Opening the door for her, he extended his hand and then helped her out. Her left heel got caught in the gravel and she sank slightly when her shoe refused to move with her.

Frank's hold on her tightened automatically and he pulled her to him.

Big mistake.

His brain instantly telegraphed the observation to him as electricity shot through his body.

Before he knew exactly what was happening, he found himself kissing her.

Under penalty of death, he wouldn't have been able

to say if he was the one who made the first move, kissing her or if she had set the ball in motion, kissing him. Either way, the next moment, their lips were pressed against each other and someone had set off an entire giant string of Fourth of July fireworks approximately three months too early.

Her mouth tasted exactly the way he'd thought it would.

Impossibly sweet, impossibly enticing.

Without meaning to, Frank deepened the kiss, wanting to savor her lips before he did the right thing and stepped back, away from her and what was clearly the line of fire. However, since his intentions were good and his plan laid neatly out before him, he thought that he could be forgiven, just this once, if he extended the time limit by a few precious seconds. He needed to absorb the sensations that were—even now—shooting wildly through him, setting off sparks and, inadvertently, a hunger that he hadn't been aware of harboring.

While it was true that he couldn't remember a time when he hadn't been attracted to women and acted on that attraction, for some unknown reason, this felt different.

Was different.

To begin with, it was going against rules, both his own and, to a lesser degree, the department's. Julianne was someone from his own department—at least she was for the time being—and that meant that there was supposed to be a hands-off policy in force.

A policy he couldn't seem to make stick.

But he would. In a minute. Maybe just a tad bit longer.

She'd never been drunk before, had sworn to herself, at a very young age as she tended to her father, that she never would be.

Because being drunk made you stupid.

Except that she didn't feel stupid. She felt, in a word, glorious. Superhuman. Right at this moment, she felt as if she could leap a tall building in a single bound and do all sorts of wonderful, incredible things.

All because he was kissing her.

No, it wasn't a kiss. The man was setting fire to her. And she didn't have enough brains to try to get away. To run for cover.

Julianne could swear that she could actually *feel* her blood rushing through her veins. Could feel her head begin to spin wildly as an unprecedented hunger began to consume her.

Was that the alcohol at work?

Or him?

Wrapping her arms around Frank's neck, leaning her body into his, she stood up on her toes and deepened the kiss.

As she did, her tongue briefly flirted with his, sending shockwaves through her body to the point that she couldn't understand how she was keeping from trembling all over.

She was a responsible woman. This *had* to stop.

In a minute.

In just another minute.

A sigh escaped her lips as, rather than stop, she kissed him harder. Kissed him with all the feeling that was running rampant through her.

This was just sex, nothing more than sex, Julianne silently insisted, even as something inside of her really craved for it to be more.

But even in her unfocused state, she knew that wasn't possible.

More was for people who won more than they lost. For people who hadn't found themselves abandoned at every turn by people they loved.

By people who were supposed to have loved her.

For her, just sex and nothing more, would have to do.

But even as she resigned herself to that, the ache inside of her grew.

Chapter 9

The heat continued to build up within her. Julianne could sense it all but consuming her. Burning the edges of her fingers and toes.

And then, suddenly, she felt hands closing down on her shoulders. Firm hands that exerted just enough force to gently push her back.

Julianne blinked, disoriented. There was space between them where, only a moment earlier, there'd been none.

Frank looked down into her face, a squadron of emotions flooding him. "Good night, Julianne."

Those were probably the hardest words he'd said in a long time. Somewhere, a medal of honor waited for him.

"You're not coming in?"

For two cents... Struggling, he shook his head. "No."

Julianne stared at him, dazed. "But I just threw myself at you."

And he would have liked nothing more than to catch her. But he knew he couldn't. Not if he wanted a clear conscience.

"Yes, you did."

And then it suddenly all became clear. "Oh." Julianne felt naked and vulnerable and every inch an idiot. This had never happened to her before. The opposite had always been true. She'd have to fight men off. "You don't want me."

Frank laughed then and shook his head. God, was she ever off base.

"Lady, you are definitely not as good at reading people as you think you are." Because they were standing outside her hotel and not inside her room, he allowed himself a second more to drink her presence— and all that could have been—in. "I don't think the word *want* even *begins* to cover what I'm feeling right now."

He wasn't making any sense. "Then why…?" Her voice trailed off as she regarded him, mystified. Was he afraid that she was trying to trap him? "I'm not expecting anything."

He laughed shortly. "Always flattering to be told that."

She waved an impatient hand at him. "You know what I mean. I'm not expecting our spending the night together to mean anything to you—to us," she corrected herself quickly, not wanting him to think that her attraction was reaching critical mass. "Isn't that what every man wants, sex with no strings?"

He would have thought so, yes. But somehow, when

she was the other party involved, it wasn't as pleasing as it should have been.

"In theory."

Her brain was in a fog. Was he trying to tell her something? Right now, subtlety was wasted on her. "And in practice?"

The smile on his lips was a fond one. She didn't want fond, she wanted passion. Fireworks. A release from all the tension she'd been experiencing.

"You're tipsy, Julianne," he told her gently. "Go in and sleep it off." Rather than kiss her again and run the risk of giving in to his baser feelings, Frank paused to brush his lips along her forehead. "I'll see you in the morning."

Frank turned on his heel and walked away. Quickly before he had a chance to change his mind—or act on a mind that was already calling him a fool.

He left her standing before the hotel, open mouthed and deeply puzzled. And torn between deep disappointment and a budding ray of admiration.

Morning crept into her system, dragging with it a really annoying headache that was not about to be ignored and an even more annoying sense of embarrassment. For a moment, she pulled the covers over her head and tried to will herself back to sleep.

Nothing happened. Because her mind launched into high gear. Throwing herself at McIntyre, what was she thinking? What the hell had gotten into her last night? she demanded silently.

And McIntyre—he'd turned her down. Was he displaying superior morals, or was it just that she wasn't to his liking?

Didn't matter. Either way, she really didn't want to have to see him today. But there was no way around it. She couldn't just not come in. After all, this wasn't her normal stomping grounds. She was a loan-out.

Okay, might as well face the music, she thought grimly, sitting up. Putting it off wasn't going to solve anything. It would only fester and grow if she hid out for the day—and the next.

Julianne dragged her hand through her long, straight black hair, wishing with all her heart that she could just as easily drag the cobwebs out of her brain and the sour taste out of her mouth.

What in God's name did people see in drinking anyway? Why would they want to deliberately wake up the next morning, feeling like sewage? A momentary surge of exhilaration the night before just wasn't worth the price.

Julianne stumbled into the shower and turned up the cold water in a desperate attempt to wake up and come to. She supposed she would have felt twice as bad this morning if they'd actually *had* sex. Grudgingly, she had to give him his due. McIntyre had saved her from that.

She supposed she should feel grateful to him. But she didn't. It was all she could do to bank down the hostility.

Frank was already in the office when she came in a little less than an hour later.

Restless, frustrated, unable to sleep more than a few minutes at a time, he'd decided he might as well come in and try to do something useful instead of tossing and turning all night, thinking of the warm mouth and warmer body he'd walked away from.

Something else to hold against this job. But even as he thought it, he knew that wasn't it. It wasn't the job that had him walking away from her last night; her judgment had been seriously impaired by the alcohol. As little as she drank, it had hit her hard. He couldn't just satisfy his own needs at her expense.

If they did wind up coming together, she would have to be clearheaded, not have her judgment clouded by either alcohol or emotions that had run rampant.

Until then, Frank mused, watching the woman walk in as if on cue, he was just going to think of her as the one who got away.

"'Morning," he called out as she passed by his opened door.

Julianne barely glanced in his direction. "Yes, it is."

And then, because there was no one else in the squad room yet, she decided to say something before the matter took on the proportions of an elephant standing in the living room, something to be acutely aware of but not mentioned.

She stopped and turned around, walking into his office. "About last night—"

He smiled at her. "You really don't drink, do you, White Bear?"

Good, she was White Bear again, not Julianne. That made talking easier. "No. But I just wanted to say—" Julianne paused. What was it, exactly, that she wanted to say?

Why didn't you want me? Why didn't you take me

when I literally threw myself at you? Is the idea of making love with me that repugnant to you?

But even as the questions formed in her mind, she knew that wasn't it. He hadn't turned her down for any of those reasons. She hadn't imagined the electricity, the chemistry that crackled between them. Hell, she could feel it now, just standing in the same room with him.

She pressed her lips together, then said, "I just wanted to say thank you."

The surprise in his eyes melt into a smile. Something inside of her said that this was far from over, which meant that she was far from out of danger. Because she could care about him. And she didn't want to care. Not about anyone. Caring only led to pain—and she'd had enough of that to last her a lifetime.

"Don't mention it," he told her, his voice low. "Just know this. The next time you do it—"

Her head snapped up as her eyes met his. "There won't be a next time," she cut in.

Frank continued as if she hadn't said anything. "—I might not be able to walk away. Consider yourself warned."

"Right." He was warning her? Did he think she couldn't take care of herself? Julianne blew out a breath, then forced herself to focus on the only thing that actually mattered, she silently insisted. "What's on tap for today?"

He glanced down at the notes he'd made to himself early this morning. "More apartments to search, more people to question. Nothing else matters until we get this creep off the streets."

Well, at least they were in agreement on that. She looked at him for a long moment, not sure how she wanted him to answer the next question. "We still partnered?"

"Yes."

Then she was going to have to dig up her A game and be on her toes at all times. "I'd better get some coffee."

He pretended that they were talking about being alert, and nothing more. "Sounds like a good idea," he told her, already turning his attention to the screen he'd pulled up on his monitor.

But as Julianne walked away, he couldn't help looking in her direction, observing the soft sway of her hips as she put distance between them.

Frank held back a sigh.

Sometimes he wondered if he was just too noble for his own good.

The tiny third-floor walk-up held the dust and grime of several tenants who had come before the victim they were investigating.

Julianne looked around with an impartial eye, deliberately leaving her emotions out of it. This was no more a home than a public restroom at a bus station. But it was the last known residence of Candy Cane, whose real name was still unknown and very possibly always would be.

Julianne couldn't help thinking of her own place, a small one-bedroom apartment she'd moved into right after joining the force. She thought of it as her haven, some place to take shelter. Periodically, she scrubbed it until it shone, determined to keep her tiny space immaculate.

No such wish here, she thought, running her hand along the bureau. The plastic gloves instantly turned grimy. Suppressing a sigh, she got down on her knees to look under the bed.

"Find anything except dust bunnies?" Frank asked a moment later, walking over to her. A search of the cupboards had yielded nothing of interest, other than telling him that the victim had a weakness for marmalade, something he himself actively disliked.

"Dust bunnies?" Julianne echoed, amused despite herself as she lowered her stomach to the floor and snaked her way under the double bed with its sagging springs. "Strange term for a head detective to use."

"Thanks to two sisters and a mother, I'm in touch with my feminine side," he cracked. He came around to her side of the bed. Only her legs were visible. "What are you doing down there?" he asked, crouching beside her. Instead of answering him, she sneezed. "Besides sneezing and getting dirty?"

He tried not to notice how firm her butt looked as the slender Mission Ridge detective undulated her way out from underneath the bed.

"Getting this," she announced, holding up a piece of crumpled paper. She sneezed again.

"Bless you." Taking the balled up paper from her, he smoothed it out. It was from a homeless shelter in the vicinity, asking for volunteers and donations. "Just a flyer," he told her.

Sitting on her heels, Julianne took the paper back from him and scanned it. Something rang a bell. "I've seen this before."

She'd gotten some dust in her hair. Leaning forward, Frank gently removed it. He heard her draw in her breath, as if the contact surprised her. Glancing at the paper again, he raised his eyes to hers.

"Where?"

"Yesterday. At the first prostitute's studio apartment. She had it on top of her TV set along with another flyer. Something from a local fast-food place." Was this finally something to connect the women? "You think it's a coincidence?"

Frank rose to his feet, offering her his hand. For a moment, she debated not accepting it, or his help, then decided that maybe, at this point, they were past playing games. Wrapping her fingers around his, she got up. And found herself standing a little too close to him for either of their own good, she thought.

Damn chemistry, anyway.

Frank regarded the flyer in her hand. "Maybe, maybe not. Both women probably lived on the street at one point or other. According to the address, this is just the closest homeless shelter. St. Vincent de Paul's Homeless Shelter," he read. "Stands to reason that they'd stay there to get a warm meal and a place to sleep."

Something about his voice didn't sound as if he was completely convinced about what he was saying. "Are you thinking what I'm thinking?"

He was thinking he wanted another chance at last night. This time around, he would have suggested she have ginger ale. And if something happened afterward when he brought her to her hotel, there'd be no reason for recriminations or acts of conscience.

What he was thinking made him grateful that the woman before him wasn't clairvoyant.

Pushing his thoughts before they took him in a whole different direction, Frank nodded. "I am if you're thinking that we should go back and get copies of the victims' pictures to show around to the staff at St. Vincent de Paul's Homeless Shelter."

A glimmer of a smile curved her mouth. "I guess then we're on the same page," she told him with approval.

"Mostly," was all he allowed himself to say before he turned around and led the way out.

The present director of St. Vincent de Paul's Homeless Shelter, Colin Wilcox, had been on the job a little less than a year. Of average height and slight build, he had a round head made that much more apparent by his swiftly receding hairline. His eyes moved like small brown marbles as he looked at the array of photographs spread out on the rickety card table before him.

If the man concentrated any harder, Julianne thought, she was certain smoke would come out of his ears. Finally, he looked up at her.

"Some of them, yes, they look familiar. But after a while—" he moved his shoulders in a vague way "—they all start to look alike. At least the ones without kids," he added hurriedly. "Kids make a difference. They tend to stick in your mind."

"Do you have some kind of sign-in list, records you keep of the people who've passed through here?" Frank prodded.

"We used to," the homeless shelter director answered.

And then he shrugged haplessly again. "But then, after a while, there didn't seem to be much point to keeping it going."

"Why not?" Frank wanted to know.

"Because all we wound up collecting were a bunch of aliases. Most of the people who stayed here were too ashamed to use their own names and some of the others, well, they hadn't heard someone say their name for so long, they just forgot it."

"These are all young women," Julianne pressed. "They wouldn't have forgotten their names." She pushed Mary's photograph in front of him. "How about this one? Do you remember ever seeing her come by? Did she ever stay here?"

Colin shook his head. "No." And then he paused, wispy eyebrows drawing together. Just as she began to pick up the photograph, Wilcox pulled it back over and studied it. "No, wait. She did," he amended. "A few months ago, I think. But she didn't have black hair. She was a blonde. Yeah, I'm almost sure of it. A blonde." Frowning, he began to look at the other photographs again, as if seeing them for the first time. "They're all blondes, aren't they?"

"One way or another," Frank commented. It was very obvious that the prostitutes were all dyed blondes, getting color out of the cheapest product they could find. The career women were another story. If they weren't natural blondes, they would have gone to salons to have their hair dyed.

"Guess California is the place for blondes," Colin murmured. His small, dark eyes darted toward the woman next to him, taking in her midnight black hair. "No offense."

"None taken," she replied, dismissing his comment. All she cared about was piecing together Mary's last few weeks. Maybe if she did, they could get that much closer to who had killed her. "So she was here? This one?" she emphasized, taping Mary's photograph when Wilcox looked as if his mind was wandering.

"Yeah, she was here. I'm certain of it now. Didn't talk much."

"What was her name?" Frank asked. Julianne looked at him, puzzled. "She might have used an alias," he explained, then looked at Wilcox, waiting. "Apparently everyone else did."

The man frowned again, trying to remember. "She had such an innocent face, I thought she was still a kid. I tried to ask her about her family, but she said they were all dead."

The comment was like a knife to her heart. Stoically, Julianne pressed, "Did she tell you her name?"

He thought for a moment. "Karen, Krystle, something like that." He shrugged helplessly. "I'm not good with names. I can't remember—no, wait," he said, his eyes widening with excitement. "I do." He looked at Julianne. "It was the same as yours."

Julianne stared at him. "What?"

Wilcox's head bobbed up and down. "Julie, that was it, she called herself Julie."

Mary couldn't stand what she'd become, so she'd fantasized about being someone else. About being her, Julianne thought.

Why did that hurt so much?

"Do you have any idea where she went when she left here?" Frank asked.

Wilcox looked at him as if he thought the detective had lost his mind. "They never tell me. Least-wise, most of them don't. The kids, though, they talk. It's like they need someone to listen to them.

"The others, the older ones, they just stop coming around. Sometimes they get a place of their own, sometimes they go to another shelter and sometimes, well, they just go," he said tactfully, but they both knew he meant that they died. He tapped Mary's photograph. "This one, though, she hardly said two words in all the time she was here. Just kept to herself. Didn't talk to the other homeless people, either."

Julianne had heard only one thing. She exchanged looks with Frank. "She was here for more than a few days?"

"Yeah, at least a couple of months." And then his eyes widened again, as if remembering caused his pupils to dilate. "Christmas," he said suddenly. "She was here during Christmas. I even caught her helping decorate the tree. Mayfair Department Store always donates one every year," he explained. "When I said something to her about what a good job she was doing, she smiled. First smile I ever saw on her. Only smile I ever saw on her," he qualified.

Yes, that sounded very much like Mary, Julianne thought. "She didn't have anything to smile about," she told the homeless shelter director quietly.

Chapter 10

At the detectives' urging, Colin Wilcox slowly re-perused the photographs of the serial killer's victims who had been prostitutes. He wasn't able to answer whether they had been there or not with any more certainty.

"Is there anyone else who works with you who might have a better memory for faces?" Frank asked, doing his best to bank down his impatience.

"We're badly underfunded," Wilcox lamented. "Most of the people who do work here are strictly volunteers—and they don't always show up when they say they will. Some of them come once or twice and then just never come back."

"I understand that—but is there any one else who's *paid* to be here?" Frank asked.

"Well, there's Jon and Suzy."

"Great. Are Jon and Suzy here?" Frank asked through gritted teeth.

"Yes."

"Could you ask them to come here?" Julianne suggested. As Wilcox ambled off, she leaned into McIntyre and whispered, "I think you have steam coming out of your ears."

Frank took a breath, letting it out slowly. "I have trouble dealing with stupid. It's a failing of mine."

For once, she understood exactly what he meant because she had the same problem. She'd grown up believing that everyone was blessed with a reasonable amount of intelligence. With age, she realized that axiom was erroneous.

She allowed herself a fragment of a smile. "Not such a failing." Wilcox returned to the room, bringing two people with him. Julianne lowered her voice. "Let's hope these two have more than half a brain between them."

As it turned out, Jon and Suzy each seemed to possess far more intelligence than their boss. After looking through the photographs, both agreed that each of the deceased prostitutes had passed through the shelter's doors at least a few times in the last nine months, although neither could be more specific than that. At least, it was a start, Frank thought as he gathered up the photographs.

None of the career women who'd been slain were familiar to either of the two shelter employees. Half was better than none.

"You're not going to say anything to the media, are you? About them being here, I mean. The dead women,"

Wilcox elaborated haltingly as he walked them to the entrance of shelter. He paused to pick up a mop that had fallen on the floor, leaning it back against the wall. He muttered something about no one knowing how to do a decent job these days, then looked at Frank for an answer to his question. "You're not, right?"

Frank had little use for the media. They tended to sensationalize everything. He believed the dead women should be allowed to rest in peace—as soon as their killer was caught.

He fixed Wilcox with a penetrating look that made the man squirm. "Why don't you want the media to know?" he asked.

Wilcox looked genuinely horrified. "That kind of publicity will keep them from coming here, the ones who need this place the most. If they think someone's watching, picking them off…" He fumbled for a conclusion to his statement and his voice just trailed off.

Frank didn't know whether to feel sorry for Wilcox or disgusted by him. The man was obviously worried about keeping his job, not the people he was supposed to be helping.

"I doubt the people who come here have the time or the opportunity to watch TV," Frank replied sarcastically.

"We do a lot of good here," Wilcox called after them. "We do."

"Jerk," Frank muttered under his breath.

"He's just afraid for his job," Julianne said, getting into the car on the passenger side. And then she looked at Frank as he got in on his side. "You think there might be two serial killers at work?"

Turning on the ignition, he pulled out of the space before glancing at her. "What?"

"Do you think there might be two serial killers?" she repeated. "One killing prostitutes, one targeting career women."

Now there was a horrific thought. "Two killers with the same M.O.? Highly unlikely." He noted the flashing red light in the middle of his dashboard. It meant a seat belt wasn't secured. "Buckle up," he instructed.

Julianne glanced down and realized her oversight. She pulled the belt over and slid the metal tongue into the slot. "Maybe they're playing tag team, like wrestlers."

Frank shook his head. There were no documented cases to support that theory—and he hoped to God there never would be. "Any time there's been a team, they've worked together. One dominant, one subservient, but always both together." Again, he glanced quickly at her to bring his point home. "And, before you say it, I don't think it's a copycat killer, either. Not all the details have been released to the press, so someone reading about the murders and deciding to go off on their own killing spree wouldn't be able to follow the M.O. to the letter."

She knew he was referring to the fact that no mention had been made that there had always been a tiny cross carved on the victim's right shoulder. That part had been deliberately left out.

Thinking, she sank deeper into her seat. "Okay, so what have we got? A rather loose connection between the prostitutes," she said, answering her own question. "How does this relate to the career women?"

"Oh, my turn?" he asked, tongue in cheek, then grew serious. "It doesn't. Yet."

The last word surprised her. "You know, when I first met you, McIntyre, you didn't strike me as the optimistic type."

He sped up in order to pass a car in the next lane, then changed lanes to get in front of it. "Just for the record, that's not optimistic, White Bear, that's tenacious."

She nodded. "So, then you're not optimistic."

"Didn't say that," he pointed out. "Just trying to clear up a point."

Okay, if it wasn't A, then it was B. "Then you *are* optimistic."

He spared her a fleeting glance even though he was driving. "Yes."

She studied his profile for a moment. It had noble lines. And, if she were to draw conclusions from last night, so did he. "About solving this case?"

She thought she saw the corner of his mouth curving. "Among other things."

Was this about last night? she wondered. Had he just pretended to be noble, in effect laying groundwork for later? To what end? He could have had her last night if he wanted. And this morning, there would have been no recriminations.

The man was complicated, she decided. "They all involve you being tenacious?"

"Yup."

Definitely complicated. She knew she was better off for not having anything happen last night, and yet…more than a little curiosity had been aroused.

And that wasn't the only thing to have been aroused.

"I see," she murmured.

"By the way, there's a party being thrown for my mother and stepfather this Saturday," he said without any preamble. "You're invited."

She ignored the invitation for the time being. "What's the occasion?"

"Their six-month anniversary." In some ways, it felt as if his mother had been married to Brian forever. Maybe because that was the way it should have been, from the beginning, he mused.

Her frame of reference when growing up had been life on the reservation. Even though it had been eight years since she'd left, she still wasn't fully acclimated to the outside world. "Do people usually throw parties for that around here?"

He thought that was an odd way to phrase it, but didn't comment. "They're not throwing it, Andrew Cavanaugh is."

She connected the name to what she'd been told previously. "The former chief of police to whose house both you and Riley have tried to get me to go."

He was unaware of Riley's efforts, but nodded. "That's the one," he replied with a grin. It was obvious that he was fond of the other man. "His parties are usually loud and noisy, but the food is incredible and you can't beat the atmosphere. Wall-to-wall cops and family," he elaborated when Julianne said nothing.

Wall to wall *Aurora* cops and family. And she was neither. "And I'm invited."

He nodded. "You're invited."

It wasn't the former police chief who was inviting her, it was McIntyre. Even if she liked parties, she wasn't about to crash one. "Andrew Cavanaugh doesn't know me from Adam."

They were at a light, and Frank gave her a very thorough once-over. One that made her feel as if her clothes had evaporated.

"Oh, he could tell you from Adam, trust me. Besides, *I* know you—and you're a cop. That's more than reason enough for an invitation."

She was about to point out that she was on loan, that she didn't belong here and that she didn't believe in crashing parties, but only got as far as the first two words.

"I don't—"

He didn't give her a chance to refuse. "What have you got to lose?" he challenged. "I'll give you the address and you can come over on your own. You don't like it, you're free to leave. Nobody's going to handcuff you to the banister."

The way he said it suggested to her that he'd considered that an option. "So that's already crossed your mind?"

"No, but I'm guessing it probably crossed yours," he countered.

Of course it did, since she said it, she thought. "Good call. Okay. Maybe," she qualified, knowing that when tomorrow came, more than likely, she wouldn't show up at the gathering.

"All I heard was *okay,*" he told her, putting her on notice.

She laughed shortly, amused. "Is this where you being tenacious comes in?"

McIntyre merely grinned at her. She had her answer.

* * *

For the rest of the day, they went over the list of St. Vincent de Paul's employees, past and present, and the handful of volunteers that Wilcox had ultimately given them. While Sanchez, Hill and Riley reexamined the late prostitutes' living quarters, she and Frank remained at the precinct, checking into backgrounds and any prior histories that the employees and volunteers might have had for any arrests or run-ins with the law.

By day's end, Julianne's frustration had grown to huge proportions.

"Other than one of the volunteers being arrested for lewd behavior on the beach almost a decade ago, the worst thing I could come up with are several unpaid traffic tickets—all belonging to Wilcox," she told Frank when he came by her desk to check on her progress—or lack thereof. "Maybe that was why he looked so nervous when we came in," she speculated.

"That," Frank allowed, "or maybe he just had a natural aversion to having the police come by to question him."

Frank leaned in to look at her screen. What he accomplished was simultaneously invading her space and clouding her thinking. In an effort to get him to move, she repositioned her monitor so that he had a better view. He remained where he was. Crowding her.

"Looking for something?" she finally asked.

He hit a key, then another. The screen changed, but enlightenment didn't come. "Yeah."

She looked from the screen to Frank. "What?"

This time, Frank did straighten up. A sigh escaped

his lips as he did so. "I don't know. Just that magical something that'll put us on the right track. I was really hoping that we had a former mental patient or someone with a history of violence in that pack. But from the looks of it, we've got nothing but average people and solid citizens." He tapped two of the names on the list on her desk. They corresponded to the two screens he'd just perused. "One's a lawyer who also volunteers his time at a free legal aid clinic in Oakland and the other's a C.P.A. who's a scout master and he used to volunteer at a soup kitchen in Santa Cruz when he lived there. Even sings in the church choir."

Perching on a corner of her desk, Frank scrubbed his hand over his face, as if that could somehow sharpen his focus, or bring something to light.

"Nothing," he repeated more to himself than to her. "Nothing."

"I think we need to get away from this for a while," Riley suggested, getting up from her desk. The day she and the other two detectives had spent had bore no more fruit than Frank and Julianne's day. "Take a break and come back fresh. Maybe something will come to us then."

The look Frank gave his sister was both skeptical and weary. "Let's hope the serial killer takes a break, too."

"After upping the kill to two? Not damn likely," Sanchez scoffed. Julianne saw Riley shoot him a dirty look. Sanchez shrugged his stocky shoulders, backpedaling as swiftly as he could. "But hey, what do I know? Anything's possible."

Frank looked at the string of dead women neatly

tacked up on the bulletin boards. His gut told him this wasn't the end of it. "That's what I'm afraid of."

She had no intention of attending the six-month anniversary party, just as she'd had no intention of showing up at Andrew Cavanaugh's breakfast table when both Riley and Frank had suggested it. It wasn't even on her mind when her cell phone rang a little before noon on Saturday. She was on her way back to McFadden Boulevard with Mary's photograph in her purse.

When she saw Frank's name on her caller ID, the first thing she thought of was that there'd been another murder.

"Where and when?" she snapped out as she got on the line.

"18931 Riverview."

She began to program the address into the car's navigational system, then stopped. She'd heard that address before. "Isn't that Andrew Cavanaugh's house?"

"Yes." She heard the smile in his voice.

Julianne sighed. For a second, she was sorely tempted just to terminate the call and keep driving to McFadden. But, technically, McIntyre was her boss. For now. She couldn't just blow him off no matter how much she wanted to.

"I thought there'd been another murder," she said impatiently. "Look, I'm in the middle of something—"

"Still trying to find out where your cousin was staying." It wasn't exactly a guess. And the silence that met his statement told him what he needed to know. "I might have some information for you along those lines."

She was instantly alert. *"Might?"* she echoed expectantly.

"Actually," Frank amended, "I do."

She wanted to demand the information, but knew that wasn't the way the game was being played. "And, let me guess, if I want it, I'm going to have to meet you at Chief Cavanaugh's house."

"Captain Randolph did send us the sharpest knife in the drawer, didn't he?"

She knew he was smirking, she would have given anything to wipe the expression off his chiseled face. She had absolutely no patience with games, or people who played them. "If this turns out to be a ploy just to get me over there—" And why it should even matter to him that she should be there left her completely baffled.

Frank stopped her before she could—he instinctively felt—begin to elaborate about the slow torture she could devise for him. "It's not. I do have some information you'd be interested in."

"About?" It was going to turn out to be something trivial—if he actually had something, which she still doubted.

"Where your cousin lived."

Four words. Just four words. And they went straight to her chest, rendering her immobile. He was probably bluffing, but she couldn't afford to just discount it. Because McIntyre was just perverse enough to actually *have* exactly what he said he had.

"And if I show up, you'll tell me?"

"Yes."

She didn't believe him. There was more of a catch to it. "Immediately?"

Julianne heard him laugh. Though she tried to block it, the sound encompassed her, warming her like a fire on a cold night. She wished it wouldn't, but there was no getting away from the fact.

It had been her hope that having sex with Frank McIntyre would have permanently laid to rest her attraction to him, but that hadn't happened. Yet.

"No, not immediately," he told her. "I want you to stay at the party for a little while."

She knew better than to agree outright. He had her over a barrel, but she still wanted to be clear on as much as she could be. "How little a while?"

She heard him pause, considering her question. "Give it two hours."

Two hours. An eternity. "And after that?"

"I'll tell you," he said cheerfully. "So, do we have a deal?"

She was already turning her car around and heading back to the hotel. "Do I have a choice?"

"Sure. You don't have to come."

Right. He knew that wasn't going to happen. For only one reason. "And you won't tell me."

"You catch on quick."

Stopped at a light, she looked down at what she was wearing: worn jeans and a T-shirt that had seen better days. She'd put them on so she'd appear nonthreatening to the prostitutes. Ordinarily, she didn't care what people thought, but she didn't want to look like a ragamuffin, either.

"I'll be there as soon as I can," she told him.

"Don't bother changing," he told her, guessing for the reason for the delay. "It's strictly casual. Come as you are."

"And if I'm naked?" she posed.

"You wouldn't be driving around in your car if you were."

"Good hearing," she commented.

"I like to keep all my parts in top running order," he quipped.

She refused to let her imagination run off with that. "Yeah, that's what they all say. I'll be there soon," she promised, ending the call with a snap of the lid on her cell phone.

When had it gotten so warm in her car?

Forty minutes later, after stopping at the hotel to put on a shirt, a long-sleeved white one that buttoned in the front and had been freshly ironed, and black, thin pinstriped slacks, then picking up a bottle of wine as a last-minute gift, Julianne showed up at Andrew Cavanaugh's residence.

The noise—music, laughter and overlapping conversations—was not fully contained by the closed door. The people inside sounded as if they were having fun. She didn't know if she was up to facing that.

For a moment, she debated just turning around and getting back into her car. McIntyre was probably putting her on about the information, using it to get her over here.

But she couldn't leave any stone unturned, Julianne silently insisted.

She forced herself to knock on the door before she

could leave. She knocked hard, instinctively knowing that the doorbell would go unheard. The moment she knocked, the door sprang open, giving her the impression that someone had been waiting and watching for her.

She expected to see Frank standing there. Instead, she found herself looking up at a tall, distinguished-looking man in his early fifties with possibly the warmest smile she'd ever seen.

He looked enough like Brian Cavanaugh to convince her that she was in the presence of the family patriarch and former chief of police, Andrew Cavanaugh. But before Julianne could say a word or introduce herself, the man was enveloping her hand warmly between both of his.

She felt both power and tranquility radiating from the contact.

"You must be Julianne."

Chapter 11

"I guess I must be." Julianne heard herself murmuring, a faint smile rising to her lips almost of its own accord. Had Frank said something to him about her attending? "How did you...?"

His eyes crinkled as his smile deepened. "I'm the former chief of police, Julianne. It was my job to know everything. I still like to keep my hand in, exercise the old brain cells every now and then." His eyes skimmed over her, taking full measure, no doubt. He made her think of an eagle, majestic and in control of all he surveyed. A nice eagle, she amended. "According to my brother, Brian, Frank and Riley speak very highly of you."

Julianne was at a complete loss as to how to respond to that. She wasn't accustomed to being confronted with compliments. Criticism, yes, she knew how to react then. But this was unfamiliar ground for her.

She cleared her throat. "Yes, well, I think they're pretty good cops, too."

Andrew smiled at her, as if to indicate that her being a good police detective hadn't been the focus of the conversations he'd been privy to. But he said nothing further along those lines.

Because she made no effort to come in, he took the lead. "Would you like to come in?" he coaxed.

She flushed. "I guess I'd better, if I want my hand back."

Andrew chuckled. "Good call." But she noticed that the former police chief didn't release her hand until she was across the threshold. Just long enough for Frank to reach them.

To reach her.

"I was beginning to give up hope," he told her cheerfully.

"Hope is something you *never* give up," Andrew told him. "Not while there's a breath left in your body." And then he winked. "Remember that." And then he turned to her again. "I'd better go see to the food. A pleasure finally meeting you, Julianne."

"Likewise," she said, still a bit dazed. Suddenly realizing that she was still holding on to the beribboned bottle of wine she'd brought, she held it out to him. "Oh, this is for the Chief and Mrs. Cavanaugh."

Andrew accepted the bottle. "Thank you. I'll be sure to let them know you brought it."

As the former chief melted into the crowd, Julianne turned around to face Frank. "*Finally* meeting me?"

She echoed the word Andrew had used. "I haven't been in town that long."

"It's all relative," Frank assured her. He subtly maneuvered his body so that she was no longer facing the door—and could escape.

Julianne looked around the large living room—and whatever she could see beyond. More than half the people there were Cavanaughs, the people she'd been introduced to at Rafferty's the first night.

"Yeah, so I noticed," she commented. There were more people in this room than on the reservation, when she'd finally left it. "You people could go off and form your own city."

Frank grinned. Figuratively, they already had. Andrew had five children, all married with families of their own. Brian had four in the same state, not to mention that when the man had married his mother, he'd inherited four more "unofficial" Cavanaughs. And his stepfather's late brother, Mike, had two offspring that he'd owned up to and three that he hadn't. That made for quite a full house.

"What makes you think we haven't?" he teased. Changing the subject as he eased Julianne farther into the room, he asked, "Would you like a drink?"

She didn't want to stay any longer than she absolutely had to. "What I'd like is that information you promised me."

She wasn't thrilled with the enigmatic smile that curved his mouth. "All in good time, Julianne. All in good time. First, let's go see about that drink."

Before she could argue with him, or accuse Frank

of luring her out on false pretenses, he floored her by taking her hand and leading her over to one of the side tables against the wall. This particular one had a bar set up on it.

His brother Zack was manning the bar, aided and abetted by a pretty dark-haired woman she heard him refer to as Krystle. By the look on both their faces, she gathered that they were more than just casually friendly. The next moment, she noticed the winking diamond on Krystle's left hand. The ring silently confirmed her suspicions.

"I see he got you to come," Zack said, offering her the same warm smile she'd seen on Frank's lips. The family resemblance was hard to miss. The same bone structure, the same black hair and intense blue eyes. "Some shindig, isn't it?" Zack raised a glass in a silent toast to his step-uncle. "Andrew Cavanaugh really knows how to throw a party."

"What's really amazing," Riley chimed in, coming up behind her and Frank, "is that Uncle Andrew can do this kind of thing at the drop of a hat—and often." She placed herself between the two couples. "You should have seen our mother's wedding reception." And then Riley rethought her words. "Come to think of it, you probably will." She grinned at her older brother and his fiancée. "I heard that he's already busy putting together Zack and Krystle's reception." There was laughter in her eyes. "Should be some blowout," Riley predicted.

"Congratulations," Julianne murmured, addressing her words to the couple behind the makeshift bar.

Frank took the bottle of beer his brother handed him without a word. He saluted his future sister-in-law with it. "My money's still on Krystle coming to her senses and making a mad dash out of town."

"No," Krystle said softly, her eyes shining as she looked at Zack the way a woman might look at her hero, Julian though. "My dashing-out-of-town days are all behind me, thanks to Zack."

Lost, Julianne looked at Frank for an explanation. "Long story," he confided, lowering his mouth to her ear. "I promise to tell it to you if you stick around long enough."

That was just it, she really wasn't planning to stick around at all. These were very nice people, but she had no real business being here. She didn't fit in. But she let Frank's words slide without bothering to correct him. She'd discovered long ago that the less she said, the less she had to be accountable for.

Making a noncommittal noise, she accepted the glass of ginger ale that Zack poured for her and subtly glanced at her watch.

Eight hours later, Frank said to her, "Okay, it's getting late and I guess it's time to go."

Seated on a sofa in the living room, Julianne looked at him in surprise. She had no idea how it had gotten to be so late. The hours seemed to have melted away and she'd been having too much of a good time to notice. That in itself, she realized, was a rarity. If she attended a party at all, she was accustomed to standing on the perimeter, observing.

That sort of thing wasn't allowed at one of Andrew Cavanaugh's gatherings. Everyone was drawn in, from the youngest to the oldest. No excuses were accepted. By anyone. Cavanaughs-by-marriage were just as apt to reel people in as the core family members—and quite possibly were even more intense about it. In the last eight hours, she'd gotten completely absorbed by the Cavanaughs, there was no other word for it.

During the course of the evening, it seemed to Julianne that every single person at the party came by at least once to talk to her. Frank's mother, Lila Cavanaugh, had spent nearly an hour with her, talking to her the way she might have talked to a daughter. There were no barriers, no awkward pauses. Everything was straightforward and friendly.

They looked very good together, Julianne observed. Lila and Brian seemed perfectly matched, as if they'd been created as a set. Julianne could easily see why they—and their children—were so happy about the union.

Happy, that was the word for them. They were all happy.

Another foreign concept, Julianne thought, trying to remember when she'd last been in that state. Nothing came to mind.

That was when Frank told her that *they* were leaving.

She glanced at him, wondering if she'd misheard. There was no *they.* She and Frank had come in separate cars. And she was quick to point out that fact right after they'd said their goodbyes and Frank mentioned something about dropping her off at her hotel.

"In case you've forgotten," she told him patiently, "I came in my own car, McIntyre."

Frank seemed utterly unfazed. "Okay, then you can

drop me off at my place," he countered without missing a beat.

"What about your car?"

His attention fully focused on her, he dismissed the question with a careless shrug. "I can always have Riley pick me up in the morning and bring me back here to pick it up."

"Why go through all that trouble?" she asked.

That was when the look in his eyes almost undid her. "Because a little extra time with you would be well worth it."

Something tightened in her stomach. She was reacting to him again. With effort, she held it in. "Are you supposed to be talking to me like that? I'm mean, you are technically my temporary boss."

"Not here I'm not." As far as he was concerned, they were equals away from the precinct. "Here I'm just Frank McIntyre, hoping to snag a few minutes alone with a beautiful woman."

Smooth, very smooth, she thought. How many women had this man sweet-talked? "That just glides off your tongue, doesn't it?"

The expression on his face was innocence personified. "Never had trouble with the truth."

Julianne rolled her eyes. He was good, very good. He sounded as if he meant what he said. But she was very aware of his reputation.

"Okay, I'll take you home," she told him, then gave him her conditions. "But only if you promise to tell me whether or not you actually have that information about where Mary lived."

Shouting a general goodbye to the room as he headed out the front door, Frank took her hand as easily as if he'd always been doing it. She did her best to ignore the warm feeling that came over her.

"I do," Frank said, answering her question.

Julianne stopped walking. Hunk or no hunk, she wasn't going to let him yank her around anymore. "I'm not taking another step until you tell me where her apartment is—or was," she corrected. God, but it was hard thinking of Mary in the past tense. She didn't think she'd ever get used to it.

He looked at her for a long moment, as if debating whether or not she meant it. He obviously decided that she did because the next words out of his mouth were, "All right, you lived up to your part of the bargain I'll live up to mine. I'll tell you where she was staying when she was murdered."

The mere mention of the word wounded her. She forced herself to focus on what he was saying.

"I want to go there," Julianne insisted as a surge of adrenaline appeared out of nowhere and found her. She felt her blood rushing in her veins, excitement skipping through her.

The look on his face was incredulous. He checked his watch. It was past eleven. "Now?"

"Now," Julianne declared firmly. There was no room for argument.

Frank sincerely had his doubts about the wisdom of going to that part of Aurora at this hour. "Why don't we wait until morning?" he suggested. "It's a really seedy part of the city." And it would only look more so with the absence of light.

But she refused to be talked out of it. This was where Mary lived. Possibly where she died. She *had* to see it.

"I'm not afraid," she told him crisply, then tried her best to smile as she added, "I have the chief of detectives' stepson with me."

Frank set his mouth grimly. "Okay."

He agreed, but it was against his better judgment. Not because the area wasn't safe, but because viewing the squalid living quarters at night would make them appear even more depressing than they already were. She didn't need that, he thought.

When they reached her car, she got in on the driver's side. "Why don't you let me drive?" he suggested. "I know where it is."

But she shook her head. She was too wired to sit quietly in the passenger seat. "You can guide me," she told him.

Resigned, Frank got in on the passenger side. Like a live version of a global positioning satellite, he doled out the directions in a modular voice as they came to each turn.

As she drove, she became increasingly aware of the changes that came over the scenery. For the most part, Aurora was upper middle class with all that entailed. But here, in the older part of the city, the moon didn't cast as bright a light. It somehow seemed darker along the more narrow streets with their aged buildings. Darker and sullenly hopeless.

Parking in the street before a graffiti-laden building that had, for the last ten months, been condemned by the city—Mary's building—Julianne tried to brace herself.

"You sure you want to do this?" Frank asked,

opening the heavy iron door that marked the entrance to the building and holding it ajar.

Julianne squared her shoulders and looked straight ahead. "I'm sure."

She wasn't prepared for this.

Coming from a reservation where poverty was the general a way of life, Julianne discovered that she was still unprepared for the levels of poverty, of hopelessness that she found within the condemned building.

The smell was appalling and she came close to gagging. The acrid odor that pervaded the dank, dark hallway, was made up of many components: urine, dead rats, garbage left out to rot and other things that were better left unidentified.

Because there was no electricity, they used the flashlight that she kept in her glove compartment to illuminate their way inside the building. The lone beam intensified the poverty.

"It's right here," Frank said, pointing to the apartment to the left of the stairwell.

Walking ahead of her, he pushed open the door that no longer had a lock on it. Frank crossed the threshold and waited for her. He shouldn't have told her. But then, she would have found out anyway. The discovery had to be made part of the report and she would have held it against him once she found out that he knew and hadn't told her.

"And she *lived* here?" Julianne whispered in disbelieving horror. In comparison, the home Mary had run away from had been a palace.

Complete with its own monster, Julianne thought cynically.

She could hardly bring herself to move out of the doorway. The single barren space, once advertised as a studio apartment, almost screamed of despair. It was completely devoid of furniture. Beyond the dirt, there was only one thing in the apartment.

An old, worn-out blanket spread out on the cracked wooden floor.

Mary's bed.

Finally moving forward, Julianne crossed to the blanket and crouched down to examine it. But even as she did so, her heart felt as if it was constricting in her chest.

"I gave this to her," Julianne said hoarsely, only vaguely addressing her words to Frank. "Years ago. It was our grandmother's. Oh, God." Her voice nearly cracked. She felt hands on her shoulders, felt Frank raising her to her feet. She turned to him. Angry, confused. Hurting. "How could she have lived like this? How could *anyone* have lived like this?" she demanded, struggling not to cry.

"There were people she could have gone to," Frank told her. "Missions. Homeless shelters. Organizations." All the places they were presently checking out for any spare information about the victims. "She chose not to. Pride?" he guessed.

Julianne shook her head. She had a better answer. "Fear. Mary was afraid of everyone," she told him. Her uncle had done that to Mary. Made her afraid to trust anyone. If you couldn't trust your own father, who could you trust?

A sob racking her lungs, she squeezed her eyes tight, trying to push back the tears. They managed to seep through her dark lashes anyway.

Seeing her this way got to him. He *knew* it was a bad idea, telling her. "C'mon," he coaxed. "You don't belong here."

"Neither did Mary," she insisted, raising her voice angrily.

"No," Frank agreed gently, guiding her out the door and down the hall to the front entrance. "Neither did Mary."

The air outside the building smelled almost sweet in comparison. She took in several deep gulps, trying to regain control over herself. He waited, then brought her over to the car.

"I'll drive," he told her.

She would have taken it as a challenge, had she any energy left to her. But she suddenly felt too wiped out, too numb to argue with him. Very quietly she surrendered her keys.

He drove her vehicle to his apartment.

Becoming aware of her location, Julianne eyed him quizzically. After what she'd just been through, she'd assumed that he'd bring her to her hotel.

"I thought you might want to talk for a while," he explained.

"No," she whispered, shaking her head. "What's there to talk about?"

"We'll find something," he promised, getting out. Rounding the hood, he came over to her side and opened the door for her. He took it as a bad sign that she made no cryptic remark about her capabilities regarding opening her own door. "At any rate, you shouldn't be alone right now."

She wanted to argue with him. To lash out at

McIntyre. At *anyone*. But instead, she merely nodded and allowed him to help her out of the car.

Unlocking the door to his ground-floor apartment, Frank brought her inside. "I can put on some coffee," he volunteered.

She was finally beginning to understand why her father crawled away from life and into the bottom of a bottle. The pain ripping her heart apart was almost too much to bear. She ignored his offer for coffee. "Do you have any whiskey?"

He thought of the bottle left over from celebrating his mother's marriage. It was on the kitchen counter, next to the canister of sugar. "Yes."

She took a deep breath, nodding. "Whiskey, then."

"No."

Julianne looked at him in surprise, wondering if she'd heard right. "What?"

"No," he repeated. He could guess at what was on her mind and he wasn't about to let her make that kind of a mistake. "That won't help you. It'll just give you a headache. Tomorrow the same feelings will be there and you'll have one hell of a killer hangover."

What kind of a man was he anyway? She stared at him, stunned. "I thought men liked getting women drunk. Hoping to get lucky."

"I don't want to 'get lucky,'" he deliberately enunciated the phrase. "I want you to be okay."

She bit her lower lip to keep it from trembling. "Well, that's not going to happen. I don't think I'm ever going to be okay again." Her voice broke in the middle of her words and she covered her mouth with her hands, trying to pull herself together and still the sobs that threatened to break out. "Oh God, Frank. Oh God," she repeated, unable to finish.

Because she was crying, he took her into his arms, trying to quiet her, trying to offer her what comfort he could.

"I know," he said softly against her hair. "I know. And I'm sorry. I'm so very sorry."

It was the worst thing in the world he could have done or said. The show of sympathy made the dam inside of her break apart into a million pieces.

Chapter 12

He made her feel safe. As if having his arms around her created some sort of a haven, was some kind of a barrier against all the hurt that the world had to offer. Knowing she shouldn't, Julianne clung to that. Clung to him.

Later, looking back, she wasn't really sure how it all happened.

One minute, she was holding on to Frank, on to the tiny fragment of peace he magically created for her. And then the next, she'd raised her mouth, salty with her fallen tears, to his.

In less than a heartbeat, the kiss sealed her to him, evolving from a quest for comfort to sheer exploding passion. Her arms went around his neck as she poured her entire soul into the kiss. Her fragile world was rocked because Frank McIntyre kissed her back the way she had never been kissed before—except, perhaps, that one time. By him.

Damn it, Frank silently cursed. Instead of easier, Julianne White Bear was getting harder and harder to resist.

This absolutely *had* to go under the heading of being close to superhuman, he thought, as he struggled to put distance between himself and her. Struggled to just separate himself from her.

It wasn't easy.

But he had to. For her sake if not for his. She wasn't thinking clearly and he couldn't allow himself to get carried away when she was like that.

Drawing his head back, he attempted to remove her arms from around his neck. "Julianne, you're upset—"

"Don't say no to me, Frank," she pleaded quietly. "Don't say no."

He had expected her to take offense and pull away. She didn't.

Frank bit back a frustrated groan, convinced he was going to hate himself in the morning for what he was valiantly trying to do tonight.

He had to keep talking until she came to her senses. "I didn't bring you here for this, Julianne."

She believed him. God help her, she believed him. With eyes and a mouth like sin, the man still had his own honorable code of ethics.

But she didn't want honorable, not tonight. If she couldn't lose herself in a bottle, then she was going to lose herself in him. She *needed* to.

"New plan, then," Julianne told him less than a half a beat before she sealed her mouth to his again.

He felt intoxicated. His head was swimming. And when he tried to draw her away a second time, the look in her eyes stopped him cold. It was a mixture of pleading and sadness. Sadness of a kind that he'd never seen before. Sadness that went clear down to the bone. Clear *into* the bone.

All he could think of was wiping that sadness away. He brought his mouth down to hers.

The next moment, he found himself engulfed in sensations running rampant through him. He felt as if he was about to burst into flame. A completely new experience for him. Considering the fact he was far from a novice with women, that was saying a great deal. He'd honestly thought there were no new experiences left for him.

To find out he was wrong was both humbling and earthshaking at the same time. The revelation didn't even involve any sort of new, exotic technique on her part. She wasn't doing anything different, anything extraordinary. She was just kissing him.

There was no "just" about it.

The mere sensation of her velvet lips against his awoke something inside of him, something that made him want to comfort her at the same time that it urged him to take solace within her.

In the eye of the storm, there was peace.

Rather than lyrical, the lovemaking that erupted between them sizzled and was close to frantic. Clothes went flying in all directions. Mouths, teeth, tongues went exploring, tasting, sampling. Glorying. And with each pass bringing a giant wave of extreme pleasure, the magnitude of which, heretofore, had not been felt or even suspected.

Frank came to realize it was his soul quaking, as close to an out-of-body experience as he would ever hope to have.

The more he kissed Julianne, the more he wanted to kiss her. Every single tempting inch of her.

His hands skimmed over her body, caressing, touching, possessing and questing until he was fairly certain he could re create her shape blindfolded. And all the while, as he was trying to deal with an expanding host of emotions, something inside of him was building up a huge head of steam, threatening an even greater eruption than he'd already experienced.

He'd never felt out of control before, not even marginally. Here he was barely holding on with his fingertips.

The very scent of her was driving him wild.

More than anything else, Julianne wanted to get lost in him, to literally disintegrate and maybe, just maybe, reinvent herself and come back as something new. Someone else. Someone who had no bad memories coloring each and every fiber of her life, casting shadows so engulfing that there was no space for happiness.

She *needed* happiness.

That's what this emotion was, Julianne suddenly realized with a start. *Happiness.* Frank had the ability to make things glow inside of her. The ability to bring happiness into her life, however briefly.

Close to breathless, Julianne felt herself scrambling

to embrace the warmth, to embrace the completely foreign sensation of well-being radiating all through her.

And then, out of nowhere, she felt herself in the midst of fireworks exploding throughout her body, beginning with her very core.

Startled, Julianne's deep blue eyes widened as she struggled to both absorb the experience and, at the same time, prolong it.

Was this what she thought it was?

Arching against him, pressing her lips together to keep a sob from escaping, she felt the heat of Frank's breath on her belly.

The explosion left her wanting more.

She grabbed his shoulders, barely getting her fingers around them as she urgently tried to pull Frank up toward her, desperately wanting to seal her mouth to his. To give back a little of what she'd received. It was only fair.

As Frank slowly snaked his body over hers, rising to her level, she saw his smile through the haze swirling around her brain. It wasn't a superior smirk, which would have all but killed her, but a smile, as if he could read her thoughts. As if he was enjoying her enjoying what he was doing to her.

Her heart slammed against her rib cage, tired of its prison.

Her breath all but gone, coming in ragged snatches, Julianne spread her legs for him, silently inviting Frank to become one with her.

Not to have sex with her, she suddenly realized, but to become one with her.

What had he done to her?

And then, there was no time for silent questions, no time to think, only to react. Frank was driving himself into her. The rhythm of life took hold as he infused her with the same melody that he was moving with. The same melody that he heard in his head.

Their rhythm of life.

The tempo increased, going faster and faster. Together, they raced toward the promise of stardust and dreams, however fleeting it might be. And then, just as the singular golden moment arrived, Frank, his hands joined with hers, kissed her.

Hard.

As if they belonged together forever.

The glow began to recede seconds after it had arrived and she struggled to hang on to it for just a little longer. If she could have, she would have pressed the feeling between the pages of a book.

A sense of sorrow moved to take its place. Sorrow because she'd never experienced anything even close to this level of excitement and passion before and was more than convinced she never would again.

When Frank shifted his weight off her, she expected him to get up and hurry into his clothes. Expected him to say something not too subtle about the fact that she should be leaving soon.

The one thing she didn't expect was for Frank to thread his arm around her and draw her closer to him. And she certainly didn't expect him just to hold her.

Moreover, she didn't expect to have the feel of his heart beating hard against hers generate such a sensation of comfort within her.

What was going on here? She had no answer.

The sound of their combined breathing was the only sound that drifted through the apartment. Confused by her feelings, by his actions, by everything that had transpired this last hour, Julianne turned toward the man who'd set her world on fire and demanded, "Aren't you going to say anything?"

Smiling, Frank brushed his lips over the top of her head and murmured, "How about those Dodgers?" The next moment he was laughing because she'd hit his shoulder with the heel of her hand. Hard. She packed quite a wallop, in more ways than one.

"Wrong thing to say?" he guessed.

She sat up then, pulling her knees up to her chest and huddling her body into almost a tight ball. She said nothing, her midnight-black hair raining down along her arm.

His amusement faded to concern. Frank sat up beside her. But when he tried to put his arm around her, she shrugged it off, making an unintelligible sound. "Julianne, are you all right?"

No, I'm not all right. I'm confused. Up is down, down is up and all I want to do is make love with you again. And again.

"What did you just do?" she demanded hotly. The question sounded as if it was a trick one, meant to trip him up. Frank didn't answer her immediately. "What did you just do?" she demanded again, more angrily this time, turning her face toward him.

Like a man trying to survive his way crossing a minefield, Frank picked his path slowly. "If you have to ask, I guess I must have done it wrong."

"Yes, you did it wrong," she accused. She felt like crying and laughing at the same time. Was she going crazy? "I *felt* something," she fairly shouted the words at him. "I'm not supposed to feel anything."

He stared at her. She couldn't be serious—could she? "Who told you that?"

"Me, I told me that," she snapped. "If you don't feel, then you're safe."

He had his answer. It was starting to make sense now. Julianne was angry at him because she'd just lost her defense mechanism.

"No," he corrected her quietly, skimming his fingertips along her face ever so lightly. "Then you're isolated—and you might as well be dead. Life is about reaching out, Julianne. About feeling. And you, lady, whether you like it or not, made the earth move for me."

She wished she could believe him. But she knew better. "Is that your usual speech?" she asked, trying her best to sound haughty and disdainful. Anything but naively trusting.

"No," he told her honestly. And then he smiled at her. It was a small, intimate smile and, like a rose-tipped arrow, it went straight to her heart. "It's okay to be afraid, Julianne."

He was reading her mind and that scared the hell out of her. Her chin shot up. "I'm not afraid," she retorted.

He saw right through her. Right through the lie, but

he allowed her to have it. "Good," he answered, "because I am."

What kind of a game was this? Men like Frank didn't admit to fear. They didn't *have* fear, not when it came to women. "You?"

In his own way, he'd played it safe all his life when it came to the fairer sex. It was time to risk something in order to win something.

Still, it took him a moment before he could. "Something just happened here that never happened before— and you scared the hell out of me."

She made no effort to bank down the smirk. "You're not going to tell me that you've never made love before, are you?"

"Oh, I've made love before," he assured her. "But I've never felt as if I wasn't in control of the situation before." His eyes skimmed over her, creating swirls of warmth throughout her body. And then he grinned. "Must have been a fluke."

If that was the way he wanted to play it, fine. "Must have."

But his eyes wouldn't release hers. And she could feel her heart accelerating again, just as it had the last time.

"Only one way to find out if it was or not," he told her.

It took her a second to realize that her breath was just sitting in her throat, stuck. She could barely squeeze the words out.

"And that is?"

Frank kissed her shoulder, sending all sorts of delicious sensations scrambling through her—again. And they all felt stronger than they had the first time. "Guess."

Julianne turned her face toward his and within a moment, there was no need to guess. Because he was showing her.

Exhausted, spent, Julianne fell back, snuggling against the space that Frank had created for her with the crook of his arm.

Incredibly, it had happened again. He'd had her climaxing, one overwhelming, breath-stealing sensation flowering into another until she thought she was going to die from the myriad sensations assaulting her body. Die willingly and happily.

Granted, she was as confused as she'd been the first time around, but this time she caught herself smiling more. Willing to accept the pleasure at its face value. The proof was that she found herself curling into him rather than into herself.

She knew it was all just temporary, all just an illusion. But for now, she wanted nothing more than to hang on to it for however short a time period she had left to her.

Was this what it was like, she wondered. To be normal? Not to be the prisoner of dark memories and a childhood that had had the blush of innocence stolen away all too soon?

If she could just pretend….

And then, the ribbon of a melody sliced through the sound of their joint, uneven breathing. The song was vaguely familiar to her, although she couldn't place it immediately.

The next moment, she heard Frank groaning. With a resigned sigh, he sat up. "That's my phone," he told her, looking around.

It was evident that he hadn't the slightest idea where his cell phone was. Frank began sorting through their clothes, trying to locate the evil instrument that had called a halt to their euphoric state.

Just as he found his pants, and, by association, his cell phone, a high-pitched ringing noise chimed in.

That was her phone.

They exchanged looks, both knowing what that meant. Neither one wanted to say it out loud, hoping that they were wrong, that their night of lovemaking wasn't being capped off by the discovery of yet another body cast off into a Dumpster.

"McIntyre," Frank announced crisply as he snapped open his phone.

"White Bear," Julianne said, following suit with her own silver phone. She fell silent, listening to the voice on the other end.

The world had found her again, she thought, pulling her out of paradise and back down to earth. She'd expected nothing less, but she'd hoped for just a little more time.

The man on the other end, Sanchez, stopped talking. He and Hill had been the first called on the scene and now they were calling in the rest of the team.

"Right," Julianne said, apropos to nothing in particular. "I'll be right there."

Frank had already ended his call. Putting the cell

phone down, he started getting dressed. When he spoke, his voice was vibrating from suppressed emotion.

"This guy isn't going to give it a rest until we get him," he speculated grimly.

Julianne merely nodded, hurrying into her clothes. She tried to assess what had just happened, but her efforts were futile. Finally, dressed, she looked at Frank.

"What do we tell people?" she asked.

He slipped his phone into his pocket, his mind charging in a dozen different directions at once. "About?"

She slanted a look at him, but he wasn't playing games, he was actually asking her. "About why we're driving in together."

That was when he looked at her. She couldn't read his expression. "The truth."

He had to be kidding. But just to be safe, she put the question to him. "That we were going at it like rabbits when they called?"

"That we went to investigate where one of the serial killer's victims lived and then stopped to get some coffee. We don't have to tell them where we stopped," he added, seeing the reluctance in her eyes. "Or what happened after we did."

She felt relieved and yet, at the same time, oddly put off. "Embarrassed?" she finally asked.

"Just trying to protect your privacy," Frank countered. He strapped his gun on, then checked to see if it was secure. "And to answer your question, no, I'm not. Why should I be?"

Julianne shrugged, trying her best to seem careless. She was about to stride past him to the door when he caught her by the shoulders and spun her around to face him. The look in her eyes was both defiant and confused.

"This isn't over, Julianne," he told her. "Not by a long shot."

"We've got a crime scene waiting for us," she countered, deliberately ignoring what he was saying.

She didn't know if what he said made her uncomfortable—or the exact opposite. All she knew was that she'd never been as confused, as conflicted as she was at this very moment. Making love with him had undone everything that she had believed to be true up to this evening. Not the least of which was the fact that she could take or leave sex—and it certainly never made her take leave of her senses before.

She couldn't claim that anymore. At least, not truthfully.

Once they were outside, he dug into his pocket. "Here—" he handed her the keys to her vehicle. "You drive."

She took the keys gladly. At least this was one thing she could be in control of. Her car.

As if that made a difference, something inside of her scoffed. Her world was jumbled up. And, she slanted a grudging look in Frank's direction, it was all his fault.

Chapter 13

According to the information found in her purse, victim number ten was Anastasia Aliprantis. She was a pharmaceutical representative for Geneva Labs who'd been with her company more than five years and had done very well for herself. Up until now.

The M.E. had determined that she'd been dead approximately thirty-six hours and that her murder had occurred at a location somewhere other than the site of the Dumpster.

Like the others, she'd been strangled but not sexually violated. Also like the others, she was blond, slender, under the age of forty and with no known family in the state.

And that was where the connection appeared to end. Again.

"Now we've got an equal number of women from

both walks of life," Frank observed with a mounting feeling of disgust. "Five of each."

He'd long since discarded the notion that the women were picked at random solely for their looks. The fact that the victims had no families in the immediate area was too much of a coincidence.

"Somehow, some way, the killer knew his victims." Frank repeated the obvious out loud for what seemed like the umpteenth time. "He studied them before he moved in for the final kill."

Hill frowned, moving out of a C.S.I.'s way as the latter searched the scene for anything out of the ordinary that could be tied to the murder. "Hey, it sounds plausible, but—"

"I know. How?" Angry at the way the killer seemed to be thumbing his nose at them, Frank looked at the assembled team. "I don't have an answer. Yet," he emphasized. But he was going to find one, he silently vowed, and soon. "So we start at the beginning. Sanchez, canvas the area. Maybe someone saw something. A car that shouldn't have been there, someone lugging a rolled up rug. *Something,* anything that stood out or struck them as off or odd. Riley," he turned to his sister, "you and Hill go to Geneva Labs and see if anyone there can shed any light on Anastasia's lifestyle after hours. Get a list of the doctors she gave out samples to on a regular basis."

Julianne looked at him. "You think this could be the work of a doctor?"

"Right now, I don't know what to think," he said honestly. "But I'm open to anything." He got back to assignments. "I'm going to check out the victim's apartment." The address he had was for a trendy part of the city, a newly built apartment complex directly across from a popular, recently expanded shopping center. "Julianne, you're with me."

Out of the corner of his eye, Frank caught his sister's badly hidden smile. Now wasn't the time to take her aside and ask questions as to what she thought she knew. Everything else, including his personal life, was going to have to be placed on hold until they got this maniac off the streets. At this present pace, it wouldn't be long before he was killing a woman a day.

"Okay, people. We'll compare notes when we get back to the precinct," he told them. "Now let's go get this bastard."

The apartment complex where Anastasia had lived boasted several pools and Jacuzzis, two fully equipped exercise rooms and a "common" area that was anything but. It was the last word in single living and Julianne sincerely doubted any space went for under three grand a month.

It struck her as a sinful waste of money.

Their latest victim's apartment was located in one of the complex's corners. It came with a view of the shopping center's imported Ferris wheel.

"My God, I didn't think anyone short of a celebrity lived like this," Julianne murmured more to herself than to Frank as the landlord unlocked the door to Anastasia's apartment.

She took a moment to look around and get her bearings. Spacious with cathedral ceilings, the split-level living quarters were completely done in white, from the rugs to the walls to the furniture.

The landlord backed away, taking his leave as he said something about needing to rent the apartment out as soon as possible.

"I feel like I'm lost in a blizzard," Frank commented with a shake of his head. Then he looked down at the floor again. "At least anything out of place will be easy to spot. I'll take the bedroom," he told her. "You take that room." He nodded toward what appeared to be a guest room. It was furnished in white as well.

The guest room doubled as an office. Maybe she'd get lucky and find something, Julianne mused. Pulling on her rubber gloves, she sat down at the snow-white desk and opened the deep, single side drawer. The drawer was heavy, filled with folders. All white, all neatly labeled. Julianne went through them one at a time.

For the most part, the folders contained current receipts obviously saved for tax purposes. Behind the folders was an array of expanding manila envelopes. Those housed tax forms from the previous years. They covered the last five. Her time with Geneva Labs, Julianne thought.

She flipped through the collection methodically and noted that four of the 1040 and 540 packets had been handled by a firm called Myers and Sons. The most recent one, however, carried the stamp of another accounting firm, Harlow & Higgins. Beneath the stamp was an all but illegible signature.

Julianne stared at it, trying to make out the person's name. She angled it for better light.

"Anything?" Frank asked, walking in. "All I found out was that our victim had a taste for expensive clothes and even more expensive lingerie—lots of it. I'm hoping you had more luck."

"Probably not," Julianne answered. She was acutely aware of the scent of his cologne as he stood behind her chair, looking over her shoulder. Trying to block it out, she held up the tax forms. "Until last year, Anastasia had her taxes done by the same firm."

Curious, Frank asked, "What happened last year?"

"She switched. I have no idea if that means anything or not." She held up the back side of the 1040 form so that Frank could get a look at the signature of the man who'd prepared it.

Tax accountants. Now there was an angle they hadn't explored. Did that sound as desperate as he thought? Frank felt as if he was clutching at straws, but who knew? Wasn't it about time that someone besides the serial killer got lucky?

He squinted at the signature, then looked at Julianne. "Who did the other women's taxes?"

She didn't remember finding any tax forms, but then, she hadn't looked. "I don't know."

They had nothing else to go on. This was as good as anything. "Let's find out."

Four trips to four different upscale apartments later, they had their answer. And a possible reason for some excitement.

Each of the dead career women had had their taxes done by the same firm as the last victim: Higgins and

Harlow. Not only by the same firm, it turned out, but also by the same senior accountant: Gideon Gifford.

"Think that's the connection between murders?" Julianne asked, almost afraid to hope as they left the last apartment.

"*Any* connection at this point could be something," he told her.

"Okay," she agreed, "Let's say it is. But how does that connect with the five prostitutes?" God, but it killed her to have to include Mary in that group. "They wouldn't even file tax forms, much less make use of an accountant."

Frank started up the car. "That's what we need to find out," he answered. He set his mouth grimly. "Maybe Mr. Gideon Gifford can shed some light on that little detail for us."

Gideon Gifford was an amiable middle-aged, slightly overweight man who wore rimless reading glasses. His somewhat faded brown hair was receding daily, leaving him with an ever expanding forehead. In the middle of wrestling with a complex computation, he seemed relieved to take a break.

His smile was wide and welcoming as the firm's administrative assistant brought them into the man's office.

Unlike the accountants who did their work while housed in small, mazelike cubicles scattered throughout the floor, Gifford had a corner office with a panoramic view of the city's skyline.

On his back wall were a number of framed photographs strategically arranged and permanently freezing

Gifford with prized clients and a number of other, famous people, one of whom Frank recognized as the last mayor of Aurora. There were also framed diplomas, one from Stanford and another from Yale's graduate school.

Next to those were plaques commemorating his selfless good works for the Boy Scouts, his local church and a several other organizations to which he'd either donated a good deal of his time or money—or both.

Gifford's desk had several more framed photographs, but these were more personal. They were of his family. A wife, two daughters and a son. There was also a dog. In all, it looked like the perfect American family.

"My wife gets the full credit for the way the kids turned out," Gifford joked. "I put in long hours and don't get to be home as much as I'd like. I'm planning on cutting back," he confided to Frank.

Frank noted that Julianne was oddly quiet and wondered why. "What changed your mind?" he asked the man, pretending to be interested.

Gifford grinned. "Heard that song the other day, the one that goes nobody ever died saying, 'I should have spent more time in the office.' It suddenly hit me that the song could have been about me."

Gifford went on talking, answering Frank's questions, including mentioning his whereabouts the nights of the deaths, and volunteering more information than was called for. And then he lowered his voice and confessed that part of his reason for wanting to cut back was because he'd realized that four of the women who'd been murdered had been his clients.

"I'm not normally superstitious," he quickly explained. "But I'm beginning to think that maybe I'm bad luck. My wife tells me I'm crazy, but…" His voice trailed off as he shrugged.

"Your wife's probably right," Frank told him easily. Because, for now, he had no more questions, just points to ponder, and because Julianne had remained silent through the entire interview, Frank said goodbye and left Gifford's office.

Julianne lengthened her stride to keep up with him as they walked out of the building.

"After a while, I started to get the impression that I was questioning the male version of Mother Teresa," Frank commented.

"Maybe that was what he wanted you to feel," Julianne suggested. She'd spent the whole time studying the man, listening to his answers. Watching his body language as he spoke. Searching for inconsistencies.

"Maybe," Frank allowed. He couldn't help wondering what was going on inside her head. "You were awfully quiet back there."

She had her own agenda to attend to. "You were doing fine without me."

No, there was more to it than that, Frank thought. He was willing to bet on it. "He had a plaque on his wall from St. Vincent de Paul's Homeless Shelter for his hours of selfless work."

Their eyes met just before she got into the car. "I know."

"You're not buying into it?" he asked.

Buckling up, she waited until Frank had gotten in before continuing. She answered his question with a question of her own. "Did you notice his eyes when he was talking?"

Looking in the rearview mirror, Frank backed out of the parking space. "No."

"I did. They were flat. Inscrutable. Eyes are supposed to be the windows to the soul—unless you don't have one."

The way she said it, Frank had the impression that she considered Gifford to belong to that group. Before he could ask what made her think so, she began telling him a story.

"I once knew a boy with eyes like that, back when I lived on the reservation." She stared straight ahead, remembering. "Richard Eagle. He was a few years older than I was at the time." She took a breath before adding, "He took extreme pleasure in torturing and killing animals."

They both knew that those were the classic signs of a budding serial killer. "What happened to him?"

"He disappeared after killing a dog that belonged to one of the tribe's elders."

Frank spared her a glance. Her expression gave nothing away, forcing him to ask, "Did this Richard Eagle run away or—?"

She had her own theories on that. The reservation was a law unto itself, and the outside world couldn't interfere.

"Nobody ever said," she told him, then added, "but if I had to guess, I think it was probably 'or.'" A hint of a satisfied smile played on her lips. It was obvious, though she said nothing more, that she thought that justice had been served.

* * *

"Gideon Gifford?" the director at St. Vincent de Paul's Homeless Shelter repeated the name less than half an hour later. His round face lit up. "Sure I know him. Gideon's one of our best volunteers. Probably *the* best one," Wilcox amended. "Shows up when he says he will. Stays later than he has to." He sighed, looking over his shoulder at the chaotic common room where several of their current homeless people were gathered. "I wish I had a dozen of him."

Not if he turns out to be who we think he is. For now, Julienne kept the comment to herself.

Frank gave voice to her thoughts, though his words were only audible to her. "You might want to change that wish."

The director wrinkled his wide forehead, apparently hearing only Frank's tone but not what he'd actually said. "What?"

Frank shook his head. "Nothing. Thank you. We'll be in touch."

The director stared after them, obviously confused as to why the detectives had come by and then only asked him about his star volunteer. Shrugging, he turned away and walked into the common room.

Frank said nothing until they were outside and sitting inside the car again. They were both thinking the same thing. He could feel the tension and excitement. Their eyes met and he was the first to say it.

"That's our connection between the victims," he declared with a note that was equal parts triumph and relief. "Gideon Gifford."

* * *

The next five hours were spent back in the squad room. Frank put himself and all the task force team members to work gathering every single available shred of information that even hinted about Gideon Gifford. But the more they gathered, the less likely it seemed that Gifford was their suspect. There was no police record, no traffic tickets. Not even a minor moving violation.

From all indications, Gideon Gifford had led an exemplary, pristine life.

Hill leaned back in his chair. It squeaked in protest as he laced his fingers together above his head and sighed in frustration.

"You sure this is the guy?" he asked Frank. "I'm about ready to believe that the man walks on water when he isn't turning it into wine." Frowning, he tapped his monitor. "He was voted Man of the Year at his church three years in a row—beating out the minister." Turning his chair around, he looked over toward Frank. "We bring this guy in for questioning, the whole community's going to be outside the precinct with torches and pitch forks."

"There *has* to be something," Frank insisted. He knew what he saw on his own screen and he knew what his gut was telling him. That the two didn't add up. There had to be *something,* however minor, that gave Gifford away. "A man doesn't just get up one day after leading a supposed model life and say, 'I think I'll become a serial killer today.'"

"Here's a thought," Sanchez volunteered, having come across the same blank wall. "Maybe this Gifford's *not* our killer."

Julianne looked up. For the most part, she'd been silent since they'd returned to the precinct, choosing instead to concentrate on searching for the needle in the haystack.

"No, he's our killer," Julianne underscored with quiet feeling.

Riley sighed. "We're going to need something beyond a gut feeling."

"Yeah, but if we start asking around about him, someone's going to tip him off and he'll go into lockdown mode," Frank pointed out, chewing on the problem that was staring all of them in the face. "If we're right—and I think we are—he's killed ten women—"

"That we know of," Julianne interjected grimly.

"That we know of," Frank echoed. "You just don't escape detection this long without being very, very thorough."

Swinging her chair around to face the man who had caused her to redefine her world last night, Julianne asked, "What do you have in mind?"

The answer was very simple. "We need to catch him in the act."

"What, tail him until he goes to kill somebody?" Riley asked.

"No." That would take too long and if Gifford thought he was being watched, he could just bolt. There was an easier, riskier way. "Now that we know his type we give him someone to focus on."

"You mean to kill," Julianne corrected.

He didn't want it put in those terms. "It's a sting."

It took her less than half a second to raise her hand. "I volunteer," Julianne offered.

Frank shook his head. "Sorry, Gifford already knows you. We can't take a chance on his realizing that we're on to him," he reminded her. "Besides, you're not his type."

He was looking pointedly at her long, black hair.

That wasn't a deterrent. She thought of Mary. "All I need is a blond wig."

"Why go with a wig when you already have a blonde?" Riley injected, flipping her hand beneath her blond hair to make it flare out.

His immediate reaction was to say no. Frank didn't want to use either his sister or Julianne, but he knew he couldn't allow his personal feelings to get in the way. This was police business and the public's welfare was at stake.

He looked at Riley. "You sure you're willing to go through with this?"

"Hell, yes," Riley said with feeling. "I want this killer off the street. Now. And if I can help to get him that way, all the better."

"I'll dye my hair," Julianne said suddenly. The other four people in the room looked at her.

"Julianne—" Frank began.

He was about to point out the reasons against it. She didn't give him a chance. "No offense, Riley, but I'm guessing you've never really been poor a day in your life."

She'd lost him. "What does that have to do with it?" Frank asked.

"Simple." She was talking to Frank now, pleading her case with passion. "She might not be convincing. I know what poverty feels like. What being desperate feels like. And most of all, I know what it means not to have anyone to turn to for support. You've always had your family," she said to Riley and then turned back to Frank. "We've only got one shot at this guy, Frank. He smells anything out of the ordinary, he's gone. Which means that he'll be free to start all over again somewhere else. I didn't say anything when we went to his office. He doesn't even know what my voice sounds like. You did all the talking," she reminded him. "Please, Frank, I wouldn't ask you if it wasn't important. I owe this to Mary. I want to nail this creep to the wall."

The word *no* hovered on his lips. But he knew if he said it, he'd be thinking with his heart, not his head. In his gut, he knew that she'd be the more convincing one. She was the one with that kind of background to draw on. It could make a difference.

His eyes swept over her and he shook his head. "Seems a shame to dye that hair."

He'd given her his answer. Julianne let go of the breath she'd been holding. "It'll grow out," she assured him matter-of-factly.

Frank sighed. It was a done deal. "Okay. We go with you. But we do it my way." He had to be able to exercise some control over the situation. In his gut, he knew it wouldn't be enough, but at least it was something.

"Sure."

Julianne had agreed much too quickly, he thought, fervently hoping he wasn't going to regret this decision.

Too late. The words materialized out of nowhere, whispering across the perimeter of his mind.

Chapter 14

The stiletto heels forced her to slow down as she made her way through the doors of St. Vincent de Paul's Homeless Shelter.

Even mindful of her balancing act, Julianne felt amazingly calm. No nerves stretching themselves to the end of their capacity, no jitters making her stomach turn somersaults. It was almost as if this was what she'd been meant to do all along.

Rid the world of a monster.

Although she was by herself as she walked into the homeless shelter, Julianne knew she wasn't alone. Somewhere out on the street, housed in a repair truck with a local cable company logo slapped on its side, Riley and Frank were listening to her every word, her every breath. She was wearing a wire. Because her clothing was of the tight, abbreviated variety, the computer tech had woven the wire into her bra.

It chafed against her skin as she breathed, but because it represented not only safety, but a way to trap Gifford, she did her best to ignore it. She kept her breathing shallow.

"Gifford, straight ahead," she murmured under her breath, letting Frank know that their target had been sighted. She knew that Frank would be antsy until she said that, despite the fact that the director had shown them a schedule earlier, which clearly specified when the senior accountant, among other volunteers, would be here at the homeless shelter.

Gifford was alone, distributing some sort of literature on vacant tables.

Julianne sauntered over to the man, instinctively imitating the way she'd assumed her cousin had conducted herself in the presence of strangers—afraid, but doing her best not to show it.

There was no hesitation as she confronted him. "Word on the street is that I can get a decent meal here." With hooded eyes, she allowed her glance to go from the top of what was left of his curly hair down to his highly polished dress shoes. "That true, handsome?"

Gifford did her one better. He looked at her for a long moment before he responded and she had the impression that she was being dissected and then put back together. Had she passed? Failed? She couldn't readily tell from his expression.

In any event, she'd been right. His eyes were flat. Flat and mercilessly cold despite the presence of a smile on his lips.

"Absolutely," he told her with no small enthusiasm. "Here, why don't you just come with me? I'll show you where the kitchen is." He began to lead the way to the back of the first floor where the kitchen with its industrial appliances was. "Is this your first time at St. Vincent's?"

"My first time in any place like this," Julianne retorted defensively. Her eyes challenged him to make something of it. When he didn't, she fixed a smile to her lips. "I've always been able to take care of myself until now. But then—" she shrugged carelessly, as if the topic was beneath her "—the economy's been rough on us working girls, too."

They'd reached the kitchen. There was no one there at the moment. Gifford walked in as if he was intimately familiar with the area. Opening the refrigerator, he took out two large pots and began to prepare a small serving of chili with rice. Last night's dinner.

Placing the dish on a silver-topped table where all the meals were usually prepared, he asked, "Where do you work?"

"Here and there." Julianne raised her eyes to his, a smirk curving her mouth. "Why? You planning on looking me up? Hoping to get some kind of a discount because you're feeding me with someone else's food?"

"Just making conversation—" He paused, as if realizing that he was short some crucial information. "What did you say your name was?"

"I didn't." Julianne deliberately waited a beat before telling him. "It's Sally."

He pulled over a stool for her. "Sally what?"

Julianne slid onto the stool. It surprised her that Gifford kept his eyes on her face the entire time. "Just Sally."

"Well, Just Sally, what does your family think about you working here and there?"

"Who knows? Who cares?" Her tone was dismissive as she shrugged carelessly and went on eating. The chili, she thought, was fairly good. "They're back in Oklahoma—if they're still around."

"So that's home?" he asked. "Oklahoma?"

"It was."

He looked at her thoughtfully. "Ever think about going back?"

She put herself in Mary's shoes, reacting to the question the way she imagined her cousin would. Recoiling from the mere suggestion.

"Hell, no. I couldn't wait to get out of there." And then, because her so-called benefactor appeared to be waiting for more, she added, "There's only my mother—and a never-ending parade of men with grabby hands."

"And there's nobody else to go back to?" Gifford prodding, a kindly expression on his face. When she didn't answer immediately, he told her, "I could front you the cost of a bus ride home if you did want to go back."

She allowed contempt to curl her lower lip. "You'd just give it to me?"

"It'd be a loan," he explained. "You pay me back when you can."

Right. Just how naive did he think she was? There was no such thing as a free lunch. But she was curious to see what he would say, so she pushed the envelope a little further.

"And if I stiffed you?"

"Just a chance that I guess I'd have to take," he told her philosophically.

Finishing the serving, she let her spoon clatter in the bowl as she set it down. Her eyes were steely as she looked at him. "I didn't think people like you really existed."

"We do," he assured her with just the right touch of humility. She could see how Mary, hungry to trust *someone* might have been tempted to believe him. "There's more of us than you think, Sally." He dug into his pocket and held out a bill. "Here, take it," he urged.

She looked down and saw that he wasn't holding out a twenty. It was a hundred-dollar bill. Was he trying to lull her into a false sense of security? That had to be it, she decided. Was this the way he'd gotten to Mary? Pretending to be a Good Samaritan?

"Use it to help turn your life around," he was saying to her.

Julianne looked contemptuously at the bill, then laughed harshly at the suggestion. "It's gonna take more than a hundred dollars to do that."

Her answer didn't faze him. "Think of it as a start, then." He urged the money on her. "Please."

She let suspicion enter her eyes. "And you don't want anything from me?"

"No."

Julianne pushed her plate back on the table. Rubbing against the surface, it squeaked. Her eyes on his, she grabbed the bill out of his hand. "Okay, then." Folding the bill into a tiny square, she pushed it into her bra. "Gotta say you're the easiest John I ever had."

"I'm not a John," Gifford answered her with feeling. "I would, though, like to be your friend."

Yeah, right. Was that how he did it? Did he offer to befriend those lost souls before he blindsided them? "Novel approach," she responded sarcastically. "Tell you what, friend, you've got yourself a little credit," she told him.

He didn't look as if he followed her meaning. "Credit?"

"Credit," she repeated. "The merchandise kind. You decide that you want a little something in exchange for that hundred dollars you just surrendered, you come find me." She was certain that her smile left nothing in doubt. "We'll talk."

For the first time, Julianne thought she saw something different in the suspect's eyes. A flare of interest? Or was that something else?

"And let's say if I did want to come find you—to see how you were doing," he qualified quickly, "exactly where would that be?"

Gotcha! "Corner of McFadden and Holloway," she told him. I'll be the pretty one."

With that, she slid off the stool slowly, making sure that Gifford got more than an eyeful of her long limbs. With a seductive smile, she tugged at the bottom of her next-to-nonexistent skirt, the action exposing more than it covered.

He looked surprised when she began to make her way to the front door again. "You're leaving?"

"Didn't come here for the bed," she told him matter-of-factly. "Just a hot meal that wouldn't cost me nothing. Wasn't half bad," she added, then nodded at him. "Thanks."

She walked out slowly, moving her hips in a timeless, hypnotic rhythm because she knew he was watching her. Leaving the storefront shelter behind her, Julianne walked down several more blocks before she turned down into an alley. She listened carefully to the sounds of the city with its passing cars. No footsteps. Gifford wasn't following her.

"Come get me," she whispered to her chest.

"Way ahead of you." She heard Frank's voice in her ear, thanks to the tiny ear bud he'd hidden there. Frank had begun to follow her the moment she'd left the shelter, taking care to keep an eye out for Gifford. The accountant had remained where he was.

Pulling up at the entrance of the alley, Frank waited for her to get in.

"By the way," he told her as she closed the door behind her, "talking to your chest is viewed as very sexy in some circles."

Julianne could feel color rising up to her cheeks. Heat marked its path. "You've got definite voyeuristic tendencies, McIntyre."

He grinned at her. "I've been told that once or twice."

Yeah, I'll bet.

"That was a hell of a great performance," Riley complimented her. "I even caught Frank checking his pockets, looking for spare bills." And then she grew serious. "You were right. That was a lot better than anything I could have done. Ever think of becoming an actress?" she posed out of the blue.

Settling into a seat, Julianne let out a long breath. She hadn't realized how tense she was until this very moment. So much for thinking she was calm, she silently upbraided herself.

"Too wearing," she commented. Turning away, she snaked her hands underneath the skimpy top and unhooked the wire. She sighed with relief as she turned back around and handed the wire over to Riley. "Got one that doesn't chafe?"

"Sorry." Riley took the tiny device from her. "I don't think they thought about that aspect when they came up with it." She looked at her brother. "Okay, now what?"

Getting up from the console that had helped them monitor Julianne, Frank crossed to the front of the van and got in behind the wheel. For now, they were returning to the precinct. He wasn't going to feel at ease until this charade was over, but he knew there was no point in saying anything to Julianne. The die had been cast.

"We wait until nightfall and then Julianne becomes a strolling hostess of the evening." Frank started up the vehicle. "With luck, Gifford will take the bait."

It turned out not to be that easy. Gifford didn't show that evening. Nor did he show the evening after that. Both nights Julianne strolled back and forth over the restricted terrain, tense and waiting while sending away more than her share of potential customers. Over the course of the two nights, she ignored a series of car horn blasts, whistles and shouted propositions of the baser variety.

All the while, she thought about Mary, about what she had to have felt during what turned out to be the last days of her life. This, and worse, was what her cousin had been faced with night after night. The very thought deadened her soul.

What had it done to Mary's?

And then one enraged would-be John charged out of his car, determined to drag Julianne into it. Watching, Frank had one hand on the door, ready to leap out of the van and come to her aid. But Riley stopped him.

"What?" he demanded.

"She can take care of herself," his sister told him. "Just watch." She indicated the screen that highlighted the corner where their camera was trained.

"What are you, too good for me?" the John demanded, shouting into Julianne's face.

It was the last thing he said in an upright position. The next second, he was flipping through the air, landing flat on his back with a thud. Before he could get up, Julianne had the heel of her stiletto pressed against his throat.

"I'm picky," she told him. "I like to choose whose money I accept." As if to make her point, she pressed the heel a little harder against his throat.

"Okay, okay, I get it." Julianne marginally withdrew her heel and the man scrambled to his feet, coughing. "Crazy bitch!" he shouted at her.

He'd no sooner roared off in his beat-up white coupe than another car drove up. This one was a pristine dark gray sedan. The exact make and model that Gideon Gifford drove.

Adrenaline instantly roared through her veins. Every nerve ending Julianne possessed went on tactical alert.

Gideon Gifford pressed a button on his armrest and

the window on the passenger side rolled down. He leaned toward the opening. There was a hint of admiration in his manner. "You handle yourself pretty well."

"He was an insulting jerk," she said with no attempt to hide her contempt. And then she smiled at Gifford. "Not like you." Leaning into the car, she gave him her most inviting smile. "Here to collect on that hundred dollars you lent me?"

"Just here to talk," he told her. Pressing another button on the armrest released all four door locks simultaneously. "Why don't you get in?"

She pretended to look around and assess the immediate area. "Well, it does look like a slow night," she commented, then shrugged. "Okay." Getting in, she turned toward him. "So, talk."

"Put your seat belt on," he instructed.

"The careful type, huh? Okay." Pulling the belt around her, she slipped the metal tongue into the slot. It clicked into place and she sat back. "So, where are we going?" she asked.

"Just for a drive." He took the car out of park and stepped on the gas. The beverage he had housed in the cup holder sloshed, but didn't spill. "Away from here."

"Okay, but you're just going to have to bring me back."

Gifford slanted a long look at her. "We'll see."

She forced a laugh. "Are you still trying to save my soul?"

"No." His voice was low, dangerous. "Can't save what you don't have."

She felt the hairs on the back of her neck standing up. Something was off. She could feel it. Was he switching persona? Just like that? "What's that supposed to mean?"

In response, Gifford gunned the engine, flying through the yellow light. "It means that you shouldn't be on this earth, taking up space. Women like you are just useless trash, ruining men's lives," he bit off. "Ruining families, just to feed your own needs."

"I don't have to listen to this," Julianne cried. She yanked on the door, as if trying to escape the way she knew Mary would have. The door refused to give. It was locked. She tried to pry up the lock, but it wouldn't budge. He'd done something to it. "Open this damn door," she demanded.

"I will. When I'm ready." Before she could say anything, he grabbed the paper cup from the beverage holder and threw the contents at her chest. The wire short circuited, burning her skin. She bit down hard on her lower lip to keep from screaming.

"That's so your friends in the van don't follow," he said in a mild voice, as if he were commenting on the weather.

He knew.

"Stop the car, Gifford!" she ordered in a voice that rang with confident authority. He only went faster. Julianne reached for the small pistol she had strapped to her inner right thigh.

Just as she did, Gifford accelerated and the car lunged forward. The next second, he threw it into reverse, speeding backward. Julianne was thrown forward, hitting her head on the dashboard, then back just as suddenly. The small revolver flew out of her hands.

She heard Gifford laughing. "Scrappy little thing,

aren't you? Knew you would be the second I laid eyes on you."

Julianne blinked to clear her eyes. Her vision was still blurred, but she tried desperately to focus and see where they were going.

Gifford was taking her out of the city, she realized with a sudden start. The northern portion of Aurora backed up to a game preserve that boasted of several kinds of wild animals, including a couple of mountain lions.

He was going to kill her there.

The terrifying thought throbbed in her head. "Stop the car, Gifford," she ordered, summoning as much bravado as she could. "Now!"

He only went faster. "Not now, *Sally.* Not when we're having so much fun," Gifford taunted, a nasty edge rising in his voice.

They were going at least eighty miles an hour. The vehicle careened through the streets, making twisting turns on what amounted to two wheels. Her fingers felt icy, even as perspiration began to slide down her back. She had to stop him.

Where was Frank?

As if reading her mind, Gifford laughed. "He's not going to come save you, Detective. Right now, Detective McIntyre and the rest of his crew are dealing with four flat tires."

Her eyes widened as she looked at the maniac next to her. He'd called her "detective."

There was nothing but contempt in his eyes as he glanced her way. "Didn't you think I'd see through your little disguise? I've got a 180 I.Q. MENSA comes to me with questions," he crowed vainly. "Which means I'm way too smart for you and those other buffoons, Detective. But it's been nice toying with you."

The nasty laugh that rose to his lips echoed throughout the vehicle.

Gifford stomped down on the gas, whizzing by the sparse traffic as if the other cars were just painted scenery.

A sick feeling seized hold of her stomach. Julianne looked in the rearview mirror. There was no cable van following them.

She was on her own.

Chapter 15

"Pick a place," Gifford told her, his voice mild as if they were just passing the time. As if he hadn't just admitted to being the serial killer who had terminated so many young women's lives.

This was surreal. Julianne felt as if she'd just fallen down the rabbit hole. "What?"

"Pick a place," Gifford repeated, his voice growing slightly strained. "Out there." He nodded toward the vast, engulfing darkness beyond the windshield. "Pick where you want to die."

"Paris."

He laughed harshly at her flippant answer. "Sorry, it's going to have to be somewhere closer than that." The smile on his lips when he glanced in her direction made her blood run cold. "You should be honored. I never told the others they only had minutes to live. They went on thinking they had forever." The malicious smile widened. "Until they didn't."

She had to keep him talking until she thought of a way out. "Why did you do it?" she demanded. "Why did you kill all those women?"

"Why not?" he countered, so coldly she almost shivered. The near-maniacal laugh drove fear through her heart and she struggled not to let it overwhelm her. If it did, she knew she was lost. "You have no idea what a rush it is," he told her, still traveling at breakneck speed. Signs of the city began to peel away as they went down a two-lane, tree-lined road. The foothills emerged in the distance. Gifford's voice swelled in volume as he spoke, the vision the words fashioned clearly exciting him. "Feeling the life draining out of someone, passing through my hands. Watching them struggle, then give in to the inevitable. Give in to *me*."

She could hear the self-importance in his voice as Gifford crowed about his accomplishments, about how the women had struggled and begged him for mercy with their eyes.

"In the last seconds of their lives I was *everything*. I was their God, their deliverer. Their entire *world*." He took a deep breath, as if awed by himself. "Just talking about it gives me a high."

Feeding his ego wasn't going to work, she thought. In his present state it would just backfire on her. "You're not going to get away with this, you know," she told him, her voice calmer than she actually felt. "They know who you are."

The laugh was contemptuous, belittling. "Won't do them any good," he promised.

Abruptly, he pulled over to the right, all but nosediving into a desolate spot. With a flip of his wrist, he cut the engine. He seemed infused with pride, unable to keep quiet. He talked, as if justifying that his audience would be dead soon.

"I've been preparing for this day ever since the beginning. After tonight, there won't be a Gideon Gifford. I've got a whole new life waiting for me." And with deliberate precision, agitating her all the more, he added, "New unsuspecting lives to cut short."

His eyes seemed to glow as he looked at her. From that moment on, Julianne was certain that she would always remember what the face of Satan looked like.

She had to do something *now*, before it was too late. Because she knew she'd run out of time.

In one swift movement, she hit the release on her seat belt and lunged at Gifford, her fingernails going straight for his eyes. He screamed in pain and outrage. But instead of backing off the way she thought he would, Gifford grabbed her by the throat. His powerful hands closed around the slender column and began to squeeze. Hard.

Julianne clawed at him. But Gifford was a great deal stronger and her own strength, fueled with outrage and anger, began to ebb away, dragging in a darkness in its wake.

Just as she lost consciousness, Julianne felt a jolt from behind and thought, just vaguely, that they'd been hit by another car.

But that wasn't possible. They were alone out here. *She* was alone out here.

The darkness won.

A heavy, dark curtain was still oppressively draped over her, but somewhere beyond that, she thought she felt someone holding her, tugging on her. Calling her name over and over again.

Air and consciousness returned simultaneously.

With a sudden gasp, Julianne bolted upright, her fists swinging. That same someone grabbed them and restrained her despite the frantic fury that propelled her. She was powerless again. He was going to kill her.

"Hold it, Champ. I'm one of the good guys, remember?"

Frank?

Frank!

Her eyes flew open—only then did she realize that they'd been closed.

"Frank!" His name came out in a grateful sob. Her emotions raw, every nerve in her body throbbing and adrenaline racing through her body, Julianne's first reaction was to throw her arms around him and cling for dear life.

Frank did nothing to discourage her. Closing his arms around her, he just held her to him, grateful beyond words that he'd been able to save her.

All around them, the backup that he'd called for were assessing and processing the near crime scene. Sanchez and Riley had taken Gifford away in handcuffs.

Still holding her, Frank breathed in deeply, absorbing Julianne's scent, silently whispering a prayer of thanks.

And then he felt her drawing back. She looked at him in confusion. "Not that I'm not incredibly grateful that you came riding to the rescue just as that sick bastard was trying to choke me to death, but how did you even know where I was?"

Frank laughed, shaking his head. He hadn't thought that she'd underestimated him that much. "You think I'd let you climb into his car without having some sort of way to track you?"

She looked down at the front of her wet peasant blouse. With a single movement, she ripped away the now-defunct wire. "I thought that was what the wire was supposed to be for."

"Some 'backup' way to track you?" he corrected. She raised her eyes to him in a silent question. "I planted a tracking device under Gifford's car while you tottered into the homeless shelter on those stilettos."

"I didn't totter," she sniffed. And then she blew out a breath. She'd been through a lot in her life, but this was the closest she'd ever come to death. When she looked at him again, there was no bravado in her eyes or her voice. "Thanks."

He wanted to tell her that there was no reason to thank him. That when he'd realized that she was no longer transmitting and alone with that maniac, fear had almost rendered him immobile.

But all he said was, "Don't mention it."

She was coming around now. Things were falling

into place. "But wait a minute, Gifford said you had four flat tires."

Frank laughed shortly. "No, but not for his lack of trying. The bastard threw a handful of tacks in the road. The van went over some of them—came close to having a blowout." He shrugged. Sometimes the good guys won. "We were just lucky."

It took all she had to bank down the shiver threatening to undo her. She knew if she gave in, she wouldn't be able to stop shaking. Julianne ran her hand tentatively along her throat. It felt sore, tender. "I was luckier."

The story, with all its gory details, hit the street in the morning edition of the paper. Julianne could have sworn she heard a collective sigh of relief coming from the city when Aurora's citizens learned that the serial killer was under lock and key and apparently would remain that way for the rest of his life. Unrepentant and proud of his deeds, in return for having the death penalty taken off the table, Gideon Gifford cheerfully recounted the history of all his murders.

The first thing he told the D.A. and his assistant, Brian's daughter Janelle Cavanaugh Boone, was that the police took a long time to catch on. With a sly, self-satisfied smile he said that there'd been more than ten victims. Ten more than ten to be precise. The first group, escaping any detection, had long since become one with the city's landfill.

He remembered all their names and surrendered them under the terms of the same bargain.

Mary White Bear's body was released to Julianne that morning. Julianne made arrangements for her cousin to be brought back to Mission Ridge. She wanted to bury her there rather than on the reservation where they'd grown up because she was fairly certain that Mary would have preferred it that way.

On her way back from the funeral parlor, Julianne stopped at a local drugstore and bought another bottle of hair dye. The woman on the box had lustrous blue-black hair. Hers, she knew, would be a flat, cartoonlike black, but at least it would be black until her own hair grew out. She didn't like being a blonde.

She applied the hair dye the minute she got back to the hotel.

Less than an hour later, she was packing. There wasn't much to take with her, she mused. At least, not in a suitcase.

She was almost finished when she heard a knock on the door. She ignored it. After all, she wasn't expecting anyone. All she wanted to do was just get back to Mission Ridge, bury Mary and go on her life.

But whoever was on the other side of the door refused to take a hint and knocked again. And then again. They weren't going away.

With a sigh, Julianne went to the door and yanked it open.

Her mouth dropped.

"It's about time," Frank said, walking in. "I was just about to use my male prowess and break it down." And then he stopped, turning around and doing a double take. "You dyed your hair back. Good. Blonde wasn't your color. I like you better this way."

It took her a second to recover. She certainly hadn't

expected to see Frank here. When she'd left the precinct, Frank had been surrounded by a huge circle of police personnel—friends as well as family. She'd assumed that he'd be there for a good while to come.

It made leaving easier, not having to say goodbye formally. Not easy, but easier.

She could only think of one reason why he'd be here. "Did I forget something?" she asked.

"Yeah. Me." His eyes held hers, saying things he knew he couldn't put into words just yet. Not because he lacked them, but because they would scare her away. "Were you just going to leave?"

She shrugged, turning back to her packing. She struggled to distance herself from him, from her feelings. "The case is closed," she replied simply. "You got the bad guy."

He looked at her incredulously. "You weren't even going to say goodbye?"

She avoided his eyes. "I'm not very good with goodbyes."

Frank deliberately moved her suitcase to the floor and sat down on the bed. "Andrew's throwing a party."

Just a hint of a smile curved her lips. Some things it seemed, Julianne thought, were dependable. "And this is news how?"

"The party's in our honor," Frank went on. "For capturing the serial killer. It's tonight."

This was fast, she couldn't help thinking, even for Andrew. "Then what are you doing here? Shouldn't you be on your way?"

"*Our* honor," Frank repeated, emphasizing the first

word. His eyes held hers. He understood her, he thought. Understood why she was running. Because, in his own way, he'd been running, too. But he wasn't running anymore. And he wasn't going to allow her to, either. "That means you, too."

No, in her mind, she'd already made the break. To go back would mean to go through it all again. She wasn't sure if she could a second time.

"That's very nice, but—"

Frank shifted so that she had to look at him. "You have some pressing place you need to be?"

Why was he making this so hard for her? He knew this couldn't go anywhere, she thought. They had no future together. All they had was the past. One wondrous night. "No, but—"

"You wouldn't want to hurt Andrew's feelings now, would you?" Frank asked, his voice coaxing her to reconsider.

As if that would happen. "I've got a feeling he's a pretty tough guy."

"On the outside," Frank agreed, keeping a straight face. "But he's soft and sensitive on the inside—just like me."

She laughed then. She couldn't help it. The man sitting on her bed wasn't exactly a marshmallow. "Yeah, right."

Not put off, Frank took her hands in his. "Well, I am. C'mon, Julianne. Come with me. Put in a little time at the party." The look in his eyes went straight to her gut. "What have you got to lose?"

Oh, so much, she thought. *I'm already losing it. Losing the ground beneath my feet.*

Giving in but still trying to save face, she offered a

careless shrug. "All right, I suppose. I'll come. But *just* for a little while."

He flashed a smile at her. She realized that he would have accepted no other answer. "Okay, let's go."

She looked down at the jeans and pullover she was wearing. It was fine for traveling, but not for a party that his family would be attending. "Like this?"

"Didn't I tell you? It's a come-as-you-are party."

Julianne sighed, surrendering. He had her out the door before she realized it. "There is no winning with you, is there?"

"Nope," was all he said.

Frank had the good grace not to let her hear him laugh.

The music came from the house before they ever walked in. Rhythmic music that shimmied under the skin and made people want to dance. This time around, as well as incredibly appetizing dishes, Andrew had also provided live entertainment. Riley played a mean guitar and Kyle, one of the triplets fathered by his late brother, Mike, did wicked things on the drum set. Together, they turned out to be greater than the sum of their parts.

People were shouting over the music and dancing, but everything stopped dead when Frank walked in with Julianne. The next moment, the abrupt silence was filled with the sound of applause.

Embarrassed, bemused, Julianne fought back the overwhelming desire to turn around and leave. "Are they always like this?"

"Pretty much, I'm told." It didn't bother Frank. After

years of treading on eggshells because of his father, it was nice belonging to a family where approval and support was the norm, not the unusual. "Why, do they make you uncomfortable?"

Oddly enough, Julianne thought, they didn't. Although she didn't like attention drawn to her, there was something genuine about the spontaneous applause and the quick statements of congratulations that followed.

"No," she told him, her voice barely audible because of the noise, "they don't."

Her answer made him smile. "That's good," he said, his smile widening. "That's good."

"Why?" Why should it matter how she felt about this? She'd be gone soon.

"Want to dance?" Even as he asked, he was already leading her to the small cleared-off space before his sister and Kyle.

He hadn't answered her question, but she shrugged in response to his. She supposed it wouldn't hurt to dance. The music was already moving her feet.

"Why not?"

"You know," he said, lacing his hand through hers and placing the other intimately against the small of her back and, ever so lightly, pressing her to him, "you've got the makings of a really good cop."

She raised her face to his. What was he getting at? "I *am* a really good cop."

"Confidence, I like that." He nodded his approval. "We could always use another good cop on the force. But you'd have to consider another department other than homicide."

Had she missed a step here? What was he talking about? "Why would I want to do that?"

"Because the force doesn't generally approve of a husband and wife working in the same department." He knew because he'd looked it up earlier today. "I guess I could be the one who switches—or, better yet, we might just run off for a secret ceremony." The tempo picked up and he went with it, twirling her around even faster. "That way we could go on working together. Vegas isn't all that far away. Although if Andrew ever finds out— and he will, trust me. The man has incredible powers of deduction—he'll insist on throwing us a wedding reception, which kills the whole secret thing—"

He was bouncing back and forth, and her head was spinning. Julianne held up her hand. "Hold it, hold it, hold it," she cried, overwhelmed. "Back up, McIntyre. Repeat what you just said."

His face was a study in innocence. "What part?"

"The husband-and-wife part."

"The force doesn't like husbands and wives working in the same department," he recited. "That part?"

He'd glossed right over it again. "*What* husband and wife?" she demanded.

He looked at her for a long moment, the rest of the room fading into the background. "Us."

Stunned, she stared at him. Somehow, she just kept on dancing without even being aware of it. "When did you even ask?"

The grin was almost sheepish. "I figured if I talked fast enough, you would have assumed I had and just go along with it."

Julianne abruptly stopped dancing. Shaking off his hand, she spun on her heel and walked away. "We haven't even gone out on a date and now you want to get married? You're crazy, you know that?" she threw over her shoulder.

"Yes I am," he agreed, hurrying after her. She was going for the front door and he was determined to cut her off. She had to hear him out. "Crazy if I let you go."

His hand on the door, he blocked her way out. She glared at him. "What makes you think you have a choice? Or a say in anything I do?"

"Hope," he answered simply. He started again, trying to make her understand. "Look, I've been out with an awful lot of women."

"So now you're bragging?" Was he trying to impress her?

"No, I'm explaining. I've been out with an awful lot of women and I never felt about any of them the way I feel about you. I know it's soon but I know what I want. When I thought that bastard was going to hurt you, I almost lost it." That had been, by far, the worst twenty minutes of his life. "Riley had to pull me off him." He'd bolted out of the car and dragged Gifford out of his vehicle, pummeling him. "If she hadn't been there, I probably would have killed him."

"So I made you want to kill him?"

"The point is—" Frank took her hands in his "—you bring feelings out of me that I didn't even know were there. Protective feelings. I love you, Julianne, and I want to spend the rest of my life proving it to you."

No, she wasn't going to let him talk her into this. She

wasn't going to let him in. She *couldn't*. Julianne shook her head. "Find someone else," she told him. "I can't love anybody."

"Why?" he demanded.

She wanted to leave, to just walk away without a word. Without opening up her wounds again. But he wasn't going to let her, was he? Not until she gave him an answer.

"Because everyone I've ever loved has left me. My mother, my father, Mary. If I don't love," she insisted, "I don't hurt."

But she had missed the most obvious argument against that. "You don't feel."

She raised her chin. "Exactly."

"I don't believe you," he said softly, his fingers skimming along her cheek, tracing a path along her jaw. He saw something flare in her eyes. "You're lying," he told her. "You do feel something. Something for me."

Julianne looked away. "Yeah, well, with any luck, I'll get over it."

Taking her chin in his hand, he made her look at him. "I'm not going to let you."

"What are you going to do about it, Pale Face?" she challenged. Even the nickname she'd used was to emphasize that they came from two different worlds

Frank didn't answer her. Instead, he brought his mouth down to hers.

The kiss was all velvet fire, burning away her barriers, swirling its way to her inner core in lightning speed.

"That's a start," she allowed breathlessly.

"Of the rest of our lives," Frank told her just before

he brought his mouth down on hers again. This time for longer.

In the distance, Andrew watched and smiled his approval. It'd been six months since he'd thrown a wedding reception. Zack and Krystle were up next.

But after that…

* * * * *

*Don't miss Marie Ferrarella's next romance,
BECOMING A CAVANAUGH, available September
2009 from Silhouette Romantic Suspense.*

RICK'S APPOINTMENT with his attorney early Wednesday morning went only moderately better than his meeting with social services the day before. The prognosis wasn't great—but at least his attorney was going to file a motion for DNA testing. Just so Rick could petition to see the child…his sister's baby. The sister he didn't know he had until it was too late.

The rest of what his attorney said had been downhill from there.

Cell phone in hand before he'd even reached his Nitro, Rick punched in the speed dial number he'd programmed the day before.

Maybe foster parent Sue Bookman hadn't received his message. Or had lost his number. Maybe she didn't want to talk to him. At this point he didn't much care what she wanted.

"Hello?" She answered before the first ring was complete. And sounded breathless.

Young and breathless.

"Ms. Bookman?"

"Yes. This is Rick Kraynick, right?"

"Yes, ma'am."

"I recognized your number on caller ID," she said, her voice uneven, as though she was still engaged in whatever physical activity had her so breathless to begin with. "I'm sorry I didn't get back to you. I've been a little…distracted."

The words came in more disjointed spurts. Was she jogging?

"No problem," he said, when, in fact, he'd spent the better part of the night before watching his phone. And fretting. "Did I get you at a bad time?"

"No worse than usual," she said, adding, "Better than some. So, how can I help?"

God, if only this could be so easy. He'd ask. She'd help. And life could go well. At least for one little person in his family.

It would be a first.

"Mr. Kraynick?"

"Yes. Sorry. I was…are you sure there isn't a better time to call?"

"I'm bouncing a baby, Mr. Kraynick. It's what I do."

"Is it Carrie?" he asked quickly, his pulse racing.

"How do you know Carrie?" She sounded defensive, which wouldn't do him any good.

"I'm her uncle," he explained, "her mother's— Christy's—older brother, and I know you have her."

"I can neither confirm nor deny your allegations, Mr. Kraynick. Please call social services." She rattled off the number.

"Wait!" he said, unable to hide his urgency. "Please," he said more calmly. "Just hear me out."

"How did you find me?"

"A friend of Christy's."

"I'm sorry I can't help you, Mr. Kraynick," she said softly. "This conversation is over."

"I grew up in foster care," he said, as though that gave him some special privilege. Some insider's edge.

"Then you know you shouldn't be calling me at all."

"Yes… But Carrie is my niece," he said. "I need to see her. To know that she's okay."

"You'll have to go through social services to arrange that."

"I'm sure you know it's not as easy as it sounds. I'm a single man with no real ties and I've no intention of petitioning for custody. They aren't real eager to give me the time of day. I never even knew Carrie's mother. For all intents and purposes, our mother didn't raise either one of us. All I have going for me is half a set of genes. My lawyer's on it, but it could be weeks— months—before this is sorted out. Carrie could be adopted by then. Which would be fine, great for her, but then I'd have lost my chance. I don't want to take her. I won't hurt her. I just have to see her."

"I'm sorry, Mr. Kraynick, but…"

* * * * *

*Find out if Rick Kraynick will ever have
a chance to meet his niece.
Look for A DAUGHTER'S TRUST
by Tara Taylor Quinn,
available in September 2009.*

HARLEQUIN
60
YEARS
of pure reading pleasure

We'll be spotlighting a different series
every month throughout 2009
to celebrate our 60th anniversary.

**Look for Harlequin® Superromance®
in September!**

THE
DIAMOND
Legacy

*Celebrate with
The Diamond Legacy
miniseries!*

Follow the stories of four cousins as they come to terms
with the complications of love and what it means to
be a family. Discover with them the sixty-year-old secret
that rocks not one but two families.

A DAUGHTER'S TRUST by *Tara Taylor Quinn*
September

FOR THE LOVE OF FAMILY by *Kathleen O'Brien*
October

LIKE FATHER, LIKE SON by *Karina Bliss*
November

A MOTHER'S SECRET by *Janice Kay Johnson*
December

Available wherever books are sold.

www.eHarlequin.com   HSRBPA09

You're invited to join our Tell Harlequin Reader Panel!

By joining our new reader panel you will:

- Receive Harlequin® books—they are FREE and yours to keep with no obligation to purchase anything!
- Participate in fun online surveys
- Exchange opinions and ideas with women just like you
- Have a say in our new book ideas and help us publish the best in women's fiction

In addition, you will have a chance to win great prizes and receive special gifts!
See Web site for details. Some conditions apply.
Space is limited.

To join, visit us at
www.TellHarlequin.com.

REQUEST YOUR FREE BOOKS!

2 FREE NOVELS PLUS 2 FREE GIFTS!

Silhouette® Romantic SUSPENSE

Sparked by Danger, Fueled by Passion!

YES! Please send me 2 FREE Silhouette® Romantic Suspense novels and my 2 FREE gifts (gifts are worth about $10). After receiving them, if I don't wish to receive any more books, I can return the shipping statement marked "cancel." If I don't cancel, I will receive 4 brand-new novels every month and be billed just $4.24 per book in the U.S. or $4.99 per book in Canada. That's a savings of at least 15% off the cover price! It's quite a bargain! Shipping and handling is just 50¢ per book*. I understand that accepting the 2 free books and gifts places me under no obligation to buy anything. I can always return a shipment and cancel at any time. Even if I never buy another book from Silhouette, the two free books and gifts are mine to keep forever.

240 SDN EYL4 340 SDN EYMG

Name	(PLEASE PRINT)
Address	Apt. #
City	State/Prov.	Zip/Postal Code

Signature (if under 18, a parent or guardian must sign)

Mail to the Silhouette Reader Service:
IN U.S.A.: P.O. Box 1867, Buffalo, NY 14240-1867
IN CANADA: P.O. Box 609, Fort Erie, Ontario L2A 5X3

Not valid to current subscribers of Silhouette Romantic Suspense books.

Want to try two free books from another line?
Call 1-800-873-8635 or visit www.morefreebooks.com.

* Terms and prices subject to change without notice. Prices do not include applicable taxes. Sales tax applicable in N.Y. Canadian residents will be charged applicable provincial taxes and GST. Offer not valid in Quebec. This offer is limited to one order per household. All orders subject to approval. Credit or debit balances in a customer's account(s) may be offset by any other outstanding balance owed by or to the customer. Please allow 4 to 6 weeks for delivery. Offer available while quantities last.

Your Privacy: Silhouette is committed to protecting your privacy. Our Privacy Policy is available online at www.eHarlequin.com or upon request from the Reader Service. From time to time we make our lists of customers available to reputable third parties who may have a product or service of interest to you. If you would prefer we not share your name and address, please check here. ☐

SRS09R

In 2009 Harlequin celebrates
60 years of pure reading pleasure!

We're marking this occasion by offering
16 **FREE** full books to download and read.

Visit

www.HarlequinCelebrates.com

to choose from a variety of
great romance stories
that are absolutely **FREE!**

(Total approximate retail value of $60)

We invite you to visit and share the Web site
with your friends, family
and anyone who enjoys reading.

Silhouette®

Romantic

SUSPENSE

COMING NEXT MONTH

Available August 25, 2009

#1575 BECOMING A CAVANAUGH—Marie Ferrarella
Cavanaugh Justice
Embroiled in a strange case, recently discovered Cavanaugh and homicide detective Kyle O'Brien is assigned an attractive new partner. Transfer Jaren Rosetti has a pull on him he can't quite explain. But when the murders hit too close to home, Kyle will do anything to protect the woman he's come to need by his side.

#1576 5 MINUTES TO MARRIAGE—Carla Cassidy
Love in 60 Seconds
To keep Jack Cortland from losing custody of his sons to their grandfather, nanny Marisa Perez proposes a unique solution—a marriage of convenience. But while passion becomes undeniable between them, someone close is trying to destroy this family. And no one can be trusted when the threat becomes murder….

#1577 MERCENARY'S PROMISE—Sharron McClellan
Determined to save her kidnapped sister from Colombian militants, Bethany Darrow enlists the help of mercenary Xavier Moreno…with a little white lie. Xavier has a mission of his own, but when he discovers Bethany's deception, can he manage to trust this woman he's come to care for like no other?

#1578 HEIRESS UNDER FIRE—Jennifer Morey
All McQueen's Men
When Farren Gage inherits a fortune from her estranged mother, she also inherits trouble. She is threatened for money by terrorists who Elam Rhule has come to Turkey to kill, and the two are thrown together in close quarters, finding it impossible to resist the chemistry they share. She'll need Elam's help and protection, but will his heart be safe from her?

SRSCNMBPA0809